GONE OFF HIS THUG KISSES

LAKIA

Lakia Presents

❀ Created with Vellum

JOIN AUTHOR LAKIA'S MAILING LIST!

To stay up to date on new releases, contests, and sneak peeks join my mailing list. Subscribers will enjoy the FIRST look at all content from Author Lakia plus exclusive short stories!
https://bit.ly/2RTP3EV

PROLOGUE

Patrice Johnson

Christmas Eve 1993

*S*itting back in the rocking chair, I cradled my whaling nine month old son in my arms as a fresh set of tears streamed down my cheeks. I didn't know why, but being a mother wasn't coming to me naturally. Samuel was the love of my life, my first son, and everything that I ever could've dreamed of, but I couldn't quiet his loud cries and didn't know what to do. My husband, Sean, was out working late as usual, leaving me alone to handle our son on my own.

Hopping up from the couch, I marched into the kitchen and grabbed the corded phone off of the counter and dialed my sister Victoria's phone number to see if she was still up. My heart was beating rapidly and the depressing thoughts seemed to be intensified tonight. I'd sucked it up and tucked my feelings for as long as I could and the voices changed to telling me to end my suffering because my son would be better off without me.

Although I expressed my feelings of inadequacy to my father, sister, and husband, the cries fell on deaf ears. My sister Victoria told me I shouldn't have laid down and had a baby if I wasn't ready to be a mother and planned to ask for help all of the time. My father told me

1

that I was strong and the storm would soon pass. I wished that my mother was still alive to help me through this because I felt like I was failing as a mother and losing my mind at the same damn time. Victoria's answering machine picked up and I spouted off my feelings into the recorder. She had one of those answering machines that played the message out loud so I prepared to spill my guts, praying that Victoria was within earshot to hear my pleas.

Samuel's cries grew louder and that shit only made me sob even louder. The voices, Samuel's crying, and my eyes felt like they were going to close at any minute. Victoria's answering machine beeped in my ear, bringing me back to reality and waking me up a little more. Clearing my throat, I tried to cease my tears before speaking but there was no use, my emotions were overflowing and spilled out of me.

"Hey sis, I... I ummm..." I paused for a moment and took a deep breath, attempting to get my sobs under control so Victoria could understand what I was saying. ***"Victoria, I really just need a little break for some sleep if you're home. I've been working all week and Samuel has been up every night crying all night so I haven't really gotten any sleep since Sunday. It's Wednesday now and the voices in my head are starting to say some dark shit and I'm trying to fight it, but I need a little help. Everybody keeps telling me that I'm strong and I will get through this but ... I don't know anymore,"*** I stopped speaking for a moment to breathe before I continued my shameless begging. ***"I really really just need you to take Samuel for a little while so I can get some sleep, that's all I want for Christmas. Sean had to work late tonight and I feel like I'm losing it, sis. Please please call me back as soon as you get this message."***

I placed the phone onto the receiver as Samuel leaned his head back and screamed to the top of his lungs while rubbing his eyes.

"It's okay lil man, we are going for a ride," I cooed, bouncing him up and down on my hip as I grabbed his baby bag and my car keys. "You love car rides so mommy is going to take you on a quick ride," I sang to Samuel on our way out of the door.

He continued crying until I strapped him into my Kia Sportage and pulled away from the duplex. Samuel was finally silent for the first time in an hour. This teething stage was a new beast and it was killing me but I felt like no one around me understood my pain. I only had my father, Sean, and my sister who couldn't relate to what I was feeling as a mother because they never walked in my shoes. Hell, I was scared to tell anyone else how I was feeling because they might try to take my baby or put me in a psychiatric facility. After the thoughts that crossed my mind tonight, I was really considering checking myself into one.

Driving around the block, I decided to ride for as long as I could in hopes that Samuel would remain asleep when I pulled him from the car. Victoria lived a few streets over in another duplex and I made my way to her house to see if she was home. Even if I didn't leave Samuel, I just needed to vent to someone. When I turned onto Victoria's street, I thought my mind was playing tricks on me. As I eased into her driveway, I received confirmation that my vision wasn't deceiving me. Sean's Mustang sat in the driveway when he was supposed to be at work.

Shaking my head, I wasn't a dumb bitch, something in the milk wasn't clean. Before they saw me or I lost the nerve, I hopped out of my truck, grabbed Samuel's car seat out of the backseat, and approached the front door. The window was open and weed smoke seeped through the net, right along with the unmistaken sound of their moans. A fresh set of tears rolled down my cheeks that were already crusty from the hour worth of tears I shed before taking Samuel for a ride. I was frozen from the cold weather and the trauma, my world shattered because my husband was fucking my sister while I was at home, sleep deprived, while caring for my nine month old son.

"Shit Vicky, that pussy there," Sean sighed.

"Yeah yeah Sean, you heard your crying ass wife on the answering machine. Put your clothes on and go see about your lil family. I swear that bitch almost ruined my nut with that voicemail."

"Man watch out. I ain't going home, I'm about to grab a sac of weed and go to the bar. You wanna slide through?"

"No, that dick got a lady tired. I'm about to shower and sleep. I want to be up to take Samuel his gift in the morning."

BOOM! BOOM! BOOM!

I heard enough of their trifling asses speaking and anything else would've just broken me more.

"You expecting somebody?" Sean whispered.

"Nah," she whispered back.

"Go see who it is," he commanded.

"Who is it?" Victoria questioned but I didn't reply. I knew her peephole was fucked up so she would have no choice but to open the door. "They ain't saying shit," she whispered.

"Move, I'll see who it is. It better not be another nigga," Sean stated before I heard a loud smack which I could only assume was him slapping her on the ass.

"Ahhh shit, Patrice... b... b... baby, what you doing here?" His stupid ass stuttered after swinging the door open.

Placing Samuel's car seat down on the ground, I barged past Sean and into the home.

"Sis, Sean just got here," her lying ass stuttered, buttoning up the skirt she was wearing. Ignoring the chatter, I marched into the kitchen and returned with a butcher's knife, charging them full speed. That's where I blacked out and I don't remember shit else that happened that night.

According to the prosecutor at trial, I stabbed Sean in the chest. I was probably aiming for his heart and praying that it broke like he crushed mine. They said once Sean was immobile, I went after Victoria who was hovering over him, attempting to apply pressure to his wound that was spurting out blood. I sliced her face twice, from the right side of her forehead to the tip of her nose and from the left side of her top lip to the right side of her chin then stabbed her a few additional times in her left shoulder. The prosecutor and evidence during the trial said I did all of this shit in front of my son then I packed him up in the car and went home like nothing happened.

CHAPTER ONE

Samuel "Streetz" Johnson

CHRISTMAS DAY 2020

Sitting next to Shadae's bubbly ass, I watched while she popped open her last gift underneath the Christmas tree. Her face illuminated with joy as she observed the aquamarine earring and necklace set. Prior to meeting Shadae, I only knew about diamonds but I quickly learned that wasn't her thing. She was deep into astrology, birthstones, and all that shit. Her birthday was March 20, 1993, just a week before mine so I quickly learned that was my birthstone as well.

"I love them," Shadae cooed.

"And I love you," I monotoned and Shadae leaned over to bless me with a kiss from her succulent lips.

Standing up, her extra ass put on her necklace and earrings then modeled around the room. I watched in awe. I loved Shadae, she was so fucking pretty with her dark skin and long natural hair bouncing all around her head.

When Shadae walked into my first period sixth grade class as a new student, her lips were the first attribute that grabbed my attention.

Going through puberty and learning what features I preferred and disliked about the opposite sex, I quickly realized that a nice set of lips and a pretty face were my thing. Half of my schedule, I shared classes with Shadae and we even had the same lunch but I didn't converse with her. Honestly, that wasn't out of the norm because I really didn't talk to anybody but my grandfather. I spent lunch time alone at a table, eating my food and listening to music on my iPod. Shadae approached my table and asked me if she could sit there. Initially, I shook my head no but she looked so damn pitiful that I spoke up and told her she could sit there but I needed her to respect my silence.

After school, Shadae claimed the seat next to me on the bus. This time, Shadae didn't ask, she plopped down next to me and I was forced to listen to her babble on about her life story. Really it was a bunch of shit I couldn't give a fuck about but I let her get her shit off. Shadae blabbed about how she moved to Tampa from Miami because her parents landed their dream jobs here at the University of South Florida and a bunch of other trivial things I didn't need to know. I was more of a listener than a talker though and she had a melodious voice that reminded me of my mom's voice when she called me from prison. Listening intently, I offered head nods periodically to assure her that I was listening despite my lack of response. I was happy as fuck that Shadae didn't try to force me to engage in the bullshit ass conversation because I would've asked her ass to move to another seat.

By the end of the ride I learned that Shadae moved into the vacant home three houses down from where I lived with my grandfather. Since Shadae's parents worked a lot, that often left her home alone and she hated being home by herself and I ain't have shit else to do while my grandfather worked long hours as a longshoreman so that's how we became cool as fuck. Eventually, I would tell her lil shit here and there about me but the thing that really got me to open up to her was the fact that both of our families have dark pasts and I think that's what helped us form a bond. Shadae was my platonic friend until three years ago when we decided that we would see where things went between us. I didn't like a lot of motha fuckas in my space and it seemed like the right thing to do since I didn't really see myself trusting anyone else.

I'd say we made the right decision because here we were at twenty-seven years old with a friends to lovers saga that I prayed would withstand the test of time because I didn't have shit to live for besides her. High key, Shadae was all I had in this world. My grandfather, the only parent I ever had, passed away from old age shortly after my high school graduation and I was now out here on my own. My father passed away three months before my first birthday and my mother killed him right in front of me so she was spending the rest of her life in prison.

I guess you could say I still had my mama because I didn't view her as an evil person, knowing the things that we know now, it's clear that she was struggling with postpartum depression at the time of the incident. If I came home and caught Shadae with another nigga, deadly consequences would definitely follow. That left me with zero room to judge my mother. Especially when she was struggling with postpartum depression at the time of the murder and I lacked the mental illness defense, I just didn't tolerate disrespect. Although I loved my mother, she was behind that wall and it didn't compare to having her out with me.

One of those dark secrets that I shared with Shadae was my parents' story and I didn't like to talk about that shit with anyone. Just know that my father didn't pull through and my Aunt Victoria lost the functioning of her left arm and will forever carry around the scars of the incident on her face. My mom sliced her up real good, twice across the face, leaving two gruesome scars. My Aunt Victoria hated my fucking guts to this day so my grandfather cut ties with her a long time ago. She was bitter about the hideous scars but shit, if I was in my mother's shoes, I would've made sure that neither of them survived that evening so Aunt Victoria got off pretty easy in my opinion.

Memories of my father were non-existent but I do possess one Polaroid picture of him from when I was about five or six months old. He was standing in front of his black 1990 Mustang with me in his arms. We were wearing matching Jordan sweatsuits and I was too busy chewing on my knuckles to focus on the Polaroid camera. I was the spitting image of my father when he was twenty-three years old, tall as fuck, black as fuck, and handsome too. Although I inherited his looks, I didn't act shit like his cheating ass. Growing up without both of my parents was enough of a lesson for me to know that I needed to treat women properly.

When it came to my mother, I visited her here and there and kept money on her books. That was still my OG and I loved her, even though I know she probably felt like I didn't. My grandfather always tried to tell her that I was short on words with everyone but she swore he was just trying to make her feel better. If only she knew the real.

If it wasn't for Shadae, I'd probably be spending Christmas day alone. Truthfully, I wouldn't even be upset with that because I loved silence and solitude. Motha fuckas loved to say they were an introvert but that was all me for real.

"Okay, I need you to open the last gift from me," Shadae bubbled, interrupting my thoughts as she shoved a long black box into my hands.

Shadae was a middle school teacher and didn't make a lot of money so her gifts were usually simple in comparison to mine but today, she had a jewelry box for a nigga. Pulling the top off of the box, I was expecting to see a necklace or bracelet but the contents halted my breathing for a moment. Looking from the box up to Shadae, I waited for her to give me confirmation that this shit was real. She was speechless so I interrupted the silence.

"You're pregnant, Shadae?" I questioned with a slight smirk because this was better than any piece of jewelry that money could buy. On the average day, I didn't do too much smiling. I made my money and stayed out of the fucking way but *this shit right here* made a nigga feel alive again.

"Yeah," she nodded her head.

At that moment, I envisioned a bright future ahead and I promise I felt something spark inside of me. Me, Shadae, my son or daughter and for the first time in a while, I'd have a family. Grinning brightly, I retrieved the pregnancy test from the gift box before hugging Shadae tightly.

"I'm six weeks and I feel like this baby is going to be the thing that helps my family accept that our relationship is real and we are in this thing for the long haul so I'm going to tell them at dinner today," Shadae detailed, throwing my jovial thoughts off.

Although the love between me and Shadae was real, her parents developed a strong hatred for me over the years. They were both deans at the University of South Florida and Shadae followed in their footsteps and joined the education field but they despised the fact that she wound up with a street nigga like me. When we were growing up, Mr. and Mrs. Peterson didn't have a problem with our friendship and welcomed me to the family with open arms but shit switched up when we crossed that line three years ago.

"Don't go over there telling them people shit," I commanded.

Although I let that shit roll off of my lips, I knew I had a slim chance of Shadae agreeing and that was gone piss me off and try to make her stay here. "You know I can't keep a secret, it was hard enough hiding it from you. If I go to dinner feeling nauseous and barely eat, my mom will probably already know what's up," Shadae expressed, hopping up from her seat. "But I will try."

"Then stay home."

"It's Christmas, I have to visit my family, Streetz," Shadae quipped. "You can come with me," she batted her eyelashes at me. I loved Shadae and would do a lot of shit for her but sitting around her family today wouldn't be one of them. There would be too many motha fuckas over there, excessive talking, and the men in her family feeling superior while assuming I'm going to answer their questions. I wasn't down to do none of that bullshit today or any day after.

"Don't be out all late and shit," I requested. The slight sense of glee I previously experienced dissipated and my unvarying tone returned.

"I won't, I'm going to eat and leave because I know they will be drinking and stuff and I won't be able to participate and that will only blow my mood," she yelled over her shoulder.

I looked down at the pregnancy test before placing it back into the box. Laying back on the leather sectional, I pulled out my phone to scroll through Amazon in search of a pregnancy keepsake box to store all of the sentimental shit we collected throughout her pregnancy. By the time I checked out the cart full of wooden boxes to hold everything from the pregnancy test to ultrasounds, the baby's teeth, and everything in between, I ordered four hundred dollars' worth of shit. Shadae strutted back out of the room dressed in a cream and maroon sweater dress with a pair of thigh high boots on her feet and a handful of gifts for her family in her hands.

Hopping up from my seat, I grabbed the gifts and trailed Shadae outside and stuffed them in her backseat. I planted a kiss on her lips before helping her into the car. "I'm pregnant, not cripple, Streetz."

"Understood," I leaned in and kissed her again.

"If you're going to be smiling like this until I have the baby, I might have to get pregnant again right afterwards. I don't think I've seen you smile this much since your grandfather passed away," she noted.

"Ain't shit to smile about," I shrugged.

"Not even me?" Shadae quizzed, anguish dancing around in her eyes.

She was right, after my grandfather passed away, it was like a dark cloud hovered over me, turning my already cold heart into an icicle, but being in this world alone will do that to you. I loved Shadae but even her contagious smile didn't make a nigga feel like he had something to smile about. This pregnancy, on the other hand, changed my entire outlook on life in the blink of an eye. I pecked Shadae's lips again, distracting her from the fact that I hadn't answered her question and closed her car door. Stuffing my hands in the pocket of my sweatsuit, I allowed the cool breeze to soothe me while I watched her bend the corner.

I spent the rest of the day on the couch watching football and thinking about the future of my family. Marriage was definitely the next step on the list and I prayed that I could convince Mr. Peterson that I deserved his daughter's hand in marriage.

CHAPTER TWO

Shadae Peterson

A FEW HOURS LATER.

*A*fter exchanging gifts and enjoying dinner my family pulled out the drinking games just as I expected. We were a pretty close knit family and everyone was at my parents' house for Christmas dinner this year. My grandparents left a few minutes ago and I was supposed to duck out with them but my older cousins caught me up in a conversation about my job. I was in the thick of my first year as a middle school science teacher and the stories I had were endless.

Now I messed around and stuck around too long. I was trying to respect Streetz's request of secrecy for the time being but my mom shoved a shot of Casamigos in my hand and told everyone to drink up. Biting my bottom lip I passed the tiny glass to my cousin Bella.

"Here drink this, I'm not in the mood to drink tonight," I whispered.

She glared at me for a moment before shouting. "Since when are you not in the mood to drink? Girl please, you pregnant ain't chu?" She quizzed and immediately slapped her hand over her mouth when she realized that her voice was elevated.

"What?" My father jolted from his seat, dropping his shot glass on the table.

"You're pregnant?" My mom queried.

"Yeah, I wanted to tell you guys with a cute pregnancy announcement," I whined now that the cat was out of the bag.

"A cute way? What's cute about this situation? You're pregnant out of wedlock with the seed of a drug dealer! The man doesn't smile, barely talks, and I've heard heinous things about him!" My dad roared. Everyone peered at him as he ranted on his short trek over to where I stood.

"Okay, Christmas dinner is over," my mom announced. She went around the room collecting everyone's shot glasses and pecking their cheeks before sending them on their way.

I was frozen in place. My father stood beside me, his chest heaving up and down rapidly, fists balled by his side while his nostrils flared. It took my mother five minutes to clear all of my cousins, uncles, and aunts out of the house before she returned to the kitchen. The characteristics my father spewed about Streetz weren't lies either; he talked to me and his business associates but that was about it.

When it came to me, I knew Streetz loved me but even I had a hard time pulling emotions out of him. We rarely went out unless it was a special occasion and if he wasn't handling business, he was in the house. That was a large part in what I loved about Streetz, he was a homebody that stayed out the way, I never had to worry about a woman coming to me as a woman because he wasn't about to speak with none of their asses. I loved Streetz through his dysfunctional closed off ways though. Then *that smile* Streetz emitted once he realized that we were having a baby was a sure sign that this would change him for the better.

"Do you hear me talking to you, Shadae?" My father roared, snapping me out of my own thoughts.

"I'm sorry, this is a lot, what did you say dad?"

"Why would you want to ruin your life like this? You just started your career, you're not married, and your mother tells me everything that y'all talk about so I know he doesn't treat you the best..."

"What?" I glared at my mother and her eyes darted towards the ground. "Streetz... I mean Samuel doesn't treat me bad. Sure we lack some affection in our relationship and he barely speaks but that doesn't mean he treats me poorly. You both know everything he's gone through in life so it shouldn't come as a surprise that he lacks some of those skills."

"And that's what you want for your baby?"

"Pascal, let me speak with Shadae in private," my mom requested. My father threw his hands up in the air and stormed out of the room, snatching the bottle of Casamigos from the table.

"Why would you tell him the things we have talked about?" I sobbed.

"I tell your father everything but he is putting a little extra on it," she detailed. "However, I do agree with your father, I don't think either of you are ready for this step. Samuel needs therapy to work through his issues and..."

"You and I both know that Streetz isn't going to agree to therapy," I cut her off.

"Then even more of a reason why you two don't need to bring a child into this unhealthy situation. You have to take Samuel for who and what he is and you and I both know that he isn't father material. Yeah he has potential to grow but I think you should save the next step of children for when that potential has fully bloomed."

Tears streamed down my cheeks and my parents both had valid points that I hadn't considered until this very moment. My mind went back to the brief conversation I had with Streetz prior to coming to my parents' house. Streetz's lack of response when I asked him if I gave him a reason to smile shattered my heart but I played it off, telling myself that was just how my man was. Mulling over this decision with my mother, she might be right.

"This isn't a *never* thing Shadae, just *not right now*. Y'all have the rest of your lives to start a family," she consoled me, gently rubbing her hair that was blown out.

"How am I going to tell Samuel that? I don't think he will agree to an abortion."

"It's your body so it's your choice. I'd just suggest that you stay here tonight and we can get the pills for you tomorrow and you can tell

Streetz afterwards. If you go home, he's going to try to talk you out of it," I offered a silent nod before erupting into a fit of tears in her arms.

As my mother suggested, I stayed at their home that evening and was surprised that Streetz wasn't blowing up my phone or beating down my parents' door looking for me. I didn't want to disappoint my parents or Streetz but the fact that he hadn't even called me said a lot. The next morning my mom secured an appointment and I took the mifepristone in the clinic before we went home.

In my feelings, I didn't reach out to Streetz because he didn't reach out to me. Twenty-four hours later I took the misoprostol and that's when the pain began. My heart hurt because maybe I read Streetz wrong. He seemed happy about the baby but I hadn't heard from him since I left the house. After the pain started, I took some pain pills, put on a pad, and went to sleep. A few hours later I woke up to the sound of glass shattering. Hopping up from the bed, I took a moment to wake up before rushing out of the bedroom.

"Where the fuck she at?! I been calling and texting her phone all motha fuckin' day and night. You let me come in here to see that she wasn't here yesterday so let's go again!" He roared, shoving my dad into the wall.

"I'm calling the police!" My mom shouted.

"Shadae!" Streetz bellowed, turning the corner. My dad jumped on his back and his small frame was no comparison for Streetz's six foot five inch muscular body. Streetz slammed my dad into the wall, forming a hole the size of my father. He turned around, the darkness in his eyes evident as he snatched my father up by the throat, squeezing him tightly against the wall. I knew my dad was struggling to breathe as he gurgled and clawed at Streetz's hands clasped around his neck.

I wanted to run and grab Streetz but I was immobile due to the intense cramping that hit me. Gripping my stomach, my eyes locked with Streetz. It was like he read my face, he *knew* without me informing him of a decision that I now regretted. I couldn't believe that he claimed to have called my phone and popped up over here yesterday. It had to have been while I was at the clinic or else I would've known and I knew now that my father didn't tell me that Streetz was looking for me on purpose.

"Streetz, please let him go so we can talk about this," I pleaded.

"You let them talk you into an abortion? So maybe I should send this nigga where y'all sent my seed." He started applying more pressure and lifted my father up so his feet were dangling in the air.

"It's my body, Streetz, and we weren't ready to have a baby! I'm not saying never, just not right now. Look how you are behaving right now," I waved towards him as I approached him. If I'm being honest, I was afraid of what he would do next. Any other time I was sure that Streetz wouldn't hurt me but this time was different, hatred flashed in his eyes when he glanced at me. "We don't need a baby right now. We are young and have so much more to accomplish. Let's grow a little more, mature, and get married then we can try again."

"Police! Sir, release that man or I will shoot!" I glanced at the doorway and my mother must've ran next door and grabbed our neighbor, Mr. Finch, who was a police officer.

The sight of the gun aimed at Streetz's head sent my heart rate through the roof and I was terrified of losing him. Unfortunately, Streetz didn't give a fuck about the gun trained on him as he strangled my father with additional force. I knew my father was headed to the other side because he stopped struggling. A loud pop, similar to a kid's party popper, went off and then a buzzing sound filled the air. I realized the gun Mr. Finch held was actually a taser gun. Streetz released the grip he had on my father and they both tumbled to the ground. My father gasped for air while Streetz shook violently.

A slew of police officers rushed inside and Streetz was swiftly arrested. The events that unfolded today were more than I could've imagined. Tearfully, I followed Streetz and the officers outside. "Baby, I'm so sorry. I promise I'll be there to bail you out as soon as they get you processed."

"Fuck you!" He grilled me and I ceased my movement because I felt that declaration in my chest.

An hour later the police took statements from my parents while I refused to answer any questions. My parents were upset about my refusal to cooperate but I didn't care. Marching back into my room once the police departed, I picked up my phone to call the bail bondsman that Streetz told me to go to if he ever went to jail. I noticed that I didn't have any bars for reception and I wasn't connected to the internet. "Mom, I need to use your phone and can you call T-Mobile, my phone doesn't have any signal and it's not letting me connect to the internet?"

"I uhhhhh, I turned your phone service off and disconnected the router so Samuel couldn't get in touch with you until after everything was done. It was for the best."

"For the best! You **knew** he would come looking for me, you **knew** he would call and talk me out of it so you sabotaged my phone," I seethed.

"It was for the best, Shadae! If you really wanted the baby, you would've fought harder to keep it, you and I both know that. Plus, look how Samuel behaves, you don't need to be tied to that thug for the rest of your life," my dad coughed. "Stop worrying about that thug and get me to the hospital. I didn't want to incur an ambulance bill but I have excruciating pain in my neck."

Snatching my mom's phone off of the counter, I exited the house and called the bail bondsman while I said a prayer. I was going to need a miracle for Streetz to forgive me. When the bail bondsman informed me that Streetz didn't have a bond, I knew I'd need more than a miracle to fix our relationship.

CHAPTER THREE

Streetz

"See Streetz, this is exactly what I was talking about this morning when you agreed to take me to dinner. I got dressed up in this phenomenal outfit," Shadae waved at herself, "just for you to be sitting here dressed in joggers with your face buried in that phone! Are you cheating on me? Did you meet another bitch while you were in prison?" Shadae's annoying ass voice interrupted my thoughts.

Everything about this bitch annoyed me now and the only reason I came out with her tonight was to feed her before ending shit between us. I was released from prison a few days ago. A nigga had to sit down for a year and a day after her bitch ass parents pressed charges on me for breaking and entering, aggravated battery, and all types of shit. Mr. Peterson's bitch ass even sued me civilly because I was unsuccessful at sending him to the grim reaper and only left him with a damaged larynx and fractured hyoid. If that bitch ass officer wouldn't have made it there to tase a nigga, he'd be in a pine box instead of walking around with a neck brace. Now I had to reimburse his bitch ass for the doctor bills plus pain and suffering. His flaw ass just didn't know he wouldn't see a dime because I was a master at hiding street money. As far as the system knew, I was a young broke nigga until I felt like paying him. Since he played a hand in killing my unborn, I didn't have any aspirations to buy property or anything like that so it wouldn't be no time soon.

Shaking my head, I kept staring at my phone while ignoring Shadae's antics. I'm happy she had her period and couldn't give up the pussy since I got home, that would've only made me feel bad about today. After four years, you would think Shadae knew what came with my black ass but it was clear that she didn't and that was even more of a reason I was ending the shit. I only kept her around because I didn't have anyone else I could trust to watch my crib, money, cars, and other shit. Otherwise, this disloyal hoe wouldn't even be sitting across from me. For the past week since I was released from prison, if she wasn't asleep, she was stomping all over my fucking nerves. Here I was trying to decipher this message from my plug in our secret code but I couldn't make the shit out because it had been a year since I had to use it and Shadae was making it harder by complaining instead of stuffing her face with that big ass plate of gumbo and catfish in front of her.

"Waiter, can you bring the check please?!" Shadae shouted in the middle of the restaurant, snapping her fingers in the air. I didn't have to look up from my phone to know that her dramatic ass garnered the attention of every other patron in 7th and Grove. I glared at Shadae, ready to curse her the fuck out because I loved coming here and she was about to get us put out.

"Go sit in the fucking car," I ordered, passing her the keys to my whip.

Shadae rolled her eyes and nudged my head before storming out of the restaurant. Shit, the lil bitch seemed to be over me too so that should make for an easier break than I expected. The waiter approached the table with our check and a nervous smile. I told him to hold up real quick while I pulled two hundred dollar bills out of the pocket of my WrldInvsn joggers and passed them back. After instructing him to keep the change I exited the restaurant, leaving the lamb chops I barely touched on the table. In my opinion, their lamb chops were the best in the city and I was ready to devour that shit but

Shadae ruined the little appetite I had with her bullshit. The brisk December air felt good as fuck once I stepped outside because I enjoyed the cold weather. Living in Florida, we didn't experience much cold weather so I was enjoying it for the next forty-eight hours because the temperature was supposed to shoot back up to the eighties tomorrow.

Walking down Seventh Avenue, I allowed my mind to wander. I loved the fuck out of Shadae but I wasn't in love with her anymore. As long as she didn't turn into a psycho bitch I would set her up to be free and find the type of nigga she felt she deserved because it clearly wasn't me. At twenty-eight years old, a nigga just wanted peace and living with the constant reminder of why I wasn't a father wouldn't cut it.

Shadae was on her *my body my choice* shit when she chose to have the abortion and her talking points were valid but that didn't mean I had to like the shit. That don't mean the abortion didn't fuck with me and it damn sure didn't mean that the short lived excitement and dreams that I had didn't destroy my already dark heart. The light poles in Ybor still adorned the Christmas lights in the last week of the year but that shit wasn't enough to lift my mood. Christmas time was probably always going to be a hard day for me. My mom killed my father on Christmas Eve and Shadae had an abortion the day after Christmas and I wound up in prison for a year and a day two days after that. Fuck the entire month of December. Before I could bend the corner I heard the waiter from the restaurant calling after me.

Turning around, I spotted him jogging in my direction. "Hey, you left your phone on the table."

Nodding my head, I accepted the phone and it immediately vibrated in my hand. With the screen face up, I didn't have to look for anything, the bullshit that would give me an easy out came to me.

Banks: You been missing for a whole two weeks. Either get rid of that nigga or I'm moving on.

Silently stalking over to my 1967 Chevy Impala, I climbed inside and pulled off without a word. When we got back to the crib, the mission was simple. Shadae ranted the entire drive home but I ain't acknowledge shit she was spitting. When we got inside I grabbed my

Nike duffle bag and neatly packed a few outfits inside before pulling down two shoe boxes and the fifteen inch safe that contained my jewelry.

"What are you doing?"

I ignored Shadae because I didn't do too much motha fuckin' talking. Once I had all of my shit, I carried it to the car and packed it into the trunk. Shadae was on my trail hiccuping and crying like she didn't have some other shit going on.

"What did I do for you to treat me like this?" Shadae sobbed, stepping in front of the driver's door.

"You handled shit when I had to sit down and I appreciate that but I'mma keep shit a buck. I can't get over that sneaky ass abortion or your parents pressing charges on me. If I see yo pops again, I'm going to snap that nigga's trachea through his spine and you gone hate me forever anyways. Hell, the only reason I ain't tossed yo lil ass out of my way is because you might turn into a police ass hoe next. We had a good run, but you're free to move on with whoever the fuck the nigga Banks is. I'll see you around," I monotoned before pushing her ass from in front of the car.

I'd rather stay in the trap house than remain under the same roof as Shadae. It's crazy how she went from my best friend to a bitch I couldn't stand the sight of. Just the sight of Shadae repulsed me now. I guess we really shouldn't have crossed that platonic line because now a nigga really didn't have a fucking soul in his corner.

CHAPTER FOUR

Zalana Moore

"See hoe, you and all of this hair is the reason why these young stylists are out here telling their clients to come with their hair braided down," Yola joked as she braided my hair down. She was referring to my long and thick 3C hair that was a lot to tackle which was why I often braided it up and threw a wig on.

"And that's exactly why I stopped fuckin' with them kitchen stichen ass hoes," I bantered. "My last stylist said she was going to have to charge me extra because my natural hair is so thick and it slows down the process. Like bitch, you already asking me to come in here washed and blow dried, now you crying about braiding my hair down too."

"Well I'm glad she fucked up because you are always welcome here and you gave us a good kee kee last time so what's the tea this week?" Yola questioned.

"Nothing, I haven't been in the streets this week. My family has been on my back about figuring out my life. AKA, they want me to go to college even though I keep telling them college just isn't for me." I sighed because this was a hot topic within my family as the year came to a close. "Tonight, we are having our New Year's Eve dinner and I know they are going to be on my ass again."

"Family dinner? I thought you were coming to King's tonight. Come turn up with us and I know I can get my husband to start paying you to come out and party with the other social media girls. You were a ball of fun the last time you were in here so I know you will be good at it. Plus, it pays lovely."

"I'm still sliding through King's. I just have to eat with my family first. Why you think I'm getting my hair done, I gotta be fine as fuck tonight. I'm only twenty-three, I have enough energy to attend my family dinner and throw this ass immediately afterwards," I lifted from my seat and gave the ladies a little show. King's was the nightclub that Yola's husband owned and it was definitely one of the littest establishments in the city. During my last appointment, Yola detailed an opportunity to earn money while partying and I wanted to see what that life was all about.

"Nah, see sit yo ass down," Yola laughed and I chilled the fuck out so she could finish up my hair in a timely fashion.

When Yola finished up with my hair, she spun around to search for her phone to take pictures of her work. Admiring myself in the mirror, Yola did her thing with this install and I was happy that her salon came across my timeline. The thirty inch buss down was giving everything it was supposed to.

"Next time you need to bring your fine ass brother up here. He said his name was Banks right?" One of the other stylists called from two chairs over. This was only my second time visiting Yo's Beauty Lounge so I wasn't well versed in everyone's names yet. During my initial visit, my Benz was in the shop getting serviced and there weren't any loaner cars available due to this stupid ass car shortage so Banks was my transportation to and from my appointment. When Banks returned to pick me up, I wasn't quite ready so he came inside to wait. I swear that nigga just loved attention from bitches because he could've stayed his lil light bright ass in the car instead of invading the shop full of women.

"Yeah his name is Banks but I definitely won't be bringing his ass back," I rolled my eyes. "I be trying to stay as far away from him as I possibly can."

"Good lawd that nigga so fine, I'd love to bring in the new year riding his face. Climbing that tree is definitely on my 2022 vision board. He had me sold when he walked in here tall and light skinned with a lil weight on him. But when I saw all of those tats on his arms and that panty dropping smile, I had to fight the urge to sit in his lap. 'Tis the season for a big boyyyyy. He's at least six seven ain't he?" She gushed as I eyed Yola's husband Dro entering the salon with a bouquet of roses.

"Ewwww," I gagged.

"Girl stop playing," Yola tossed over her shoulder while rummaging through her purse. "You probably hear shit like that all the time because your brother is fine as fuck. I noticed he had to dip his head a little when he walked through the door. You're pretty tall yourself so it must run in the family. How tall is he?"

Yola's back was turned so she didn't see her husband enter the shop as she spoke. Dro stepped behind her and eased his right arm across Yola's shoulder until he was gripping her neck. The lustful stare they shared through the mirror gave me hope for true love. Leaning in, he tried to whisper in her ear but I still heard that shit.

"Come to the back so I can punish yo ass, I thought I made myself clear that you only had eyes for me. These other niggas broke and ugly," he commanded. Dro applied additional pressure to Yola's neck before he slapped her ass and the involuntary moan she emitted definitely wasn't work appropriate. My ass just knew they had some kinky rough sex and my vivid imagination ran wild.

"Sparkle, take a few pictures of Zalana's hair for me please," Yola requested, leading Dro to the back with his hand clasped firmly around her neck.

I peeped that Yola was trying to hide his hard dick but my nosey ass wanted to see what he was working with. With all that ass on Yola I just knew Dro's dick was big for him to keep her satisfied. As a proud card holding member of the fat ass committee, I knew that the size of the dick mattered if he thought he was going to hit it from the back. Ugh, I rolled my eyes at my damn self and the freaky shit I thought about. Since my parents bought me a townhouse downtown right next door to my brother last year, I hadn't had sex and the toys only provide so much sexual gratification.

Sparkle came over and snapped a few pictures and I posed for the

23

pictures before exiting the shop. I loved the fact that this was a one stop shop. My nails and hair were done now all I had to do was my makeup. There were makeup artists as well but I needed a nap so having my makeup done would've been a waste of time. Pulling my Benz into my three car garage, I was excited to be home so I could shower, take a catnap, and transform into a bad bitch. Pampering myself all day was exhausting.

The garage door beeped once it was closed, signaling that the security alarm was set. Gripping my shopping bags and Gucci purse off of the passenger seat, I headed for the stairs. Entering my townhouse, I exhaled deeply when I spotted Banks seated on my couch. He was dressed in his pajamas, eating a bowl of leftover lasagna that I made last night as if this was his spot. I chuckled to myself because Banks always looked like a giant stretched out on my furniture because he was six-ten and too damn big for my shit.

"The fuck you laughing for?"

"You just so damn big up in here," I cackled although I was perturbed that he was in my shit without my permission and eating my food.

This right here was exactly why I was forced into abstinence, his black ass didn't know what space or boundaries were when it came to me. Popping up at my house all hours of the night to talk, coming in my shit to eat and everything else under the sun. I felt like I was still living at home with Banks as my next door neighbor. The only difference was he had to go outside of his house and trek across a short strip of grass to accost me. At least when we were growing up, Banks had to knock on my door to enter but now he used his emergency key like this was his crib.

When our parents gifted us these townhomes on Davis Island last year, I absolutely loved them. I mean the four bedroom three and a half bathroom townhome boasted four stories and 5,436 square feet. My humble abode was everything I could've imagined in a home that was given to me debt free with my name on the deed. The luxury feel, open floor plan, gourmet kitchen, hardwood floors, floor to ceiling windows, and private elevator in this place were perfect.

On the first floor, I had a three car garage and storage area. The second and third floors were the traditional living areas that contained the bedrooms, living room, and things of that nature and on the fourth floor, I had a gym, bar, and outdoor lounge area that overlooked the Seddon Channel. I think the fourth floor was my favorite aspect of my home because it was extremely relaxing to sip a glass of wine while overlooking the water.

Although I loved my home, I wished that they wouldn't have bought our homes right next door to each other. Low key, I believe my parents purchased these neighboring townhomes so Banks could be all up in my business. I don't think I knew a bigger snitch than this nigga. He'd plead the fifth at trial and take a ten year bid for his niggas, but if I did something he didn't agree with, his was running to our parents to snitch me out.

"How many times do I have to say that the key is for emergencies only?" I quizzed, easing my feet out of my Gucci slides.

"I was hungry and they be taxin' with these UberEats and delivery fees plus you gotta tip them too. Fuck that. I always gotta come over here to see if yo ass cooked before I pay all of that bullshit. I'm happier than a motha fucka that I did too because you throw down when it come to lasagna," he explained before shoveling another spoonful of food into his mouth.

"You really get on my nerves when you act broke," I rolled my eyes. "You know how to cook, go to the fuckin' grocery store and prepare your own meal instead of rummaging through my refrigerator like a fucking bum." Mushing Banks' head on my way past him towards the elevator, I didn't have shit else to say, I was tired.

Four hours later I woke up from my nap to find that Banks let himself out of my home and I was ecstatic about that. Not only would he come over here to eat up all of my damn food, but he would also watch tv over here as if he didn't have the same ninety-eight inch flat screen mounted on his living room wall. I had to ask his ass to turn the tv down before I climbed in my bed to nap and that still wasn't enough to give him the hint to take his ass home. We might as well have been roommates at this point. The day that he settled down and found a woman to keep him out of my space, I'd gift her a nice lil Chanel bag.

Rummaging through my designer closet, it took me a moment to finalize my outfit for the evening. I needed something sexy but not too revealing because I was going straight to the club after our annual New Year's Eve dinner with my parents. Pulling a black, feather trimmed, one shoulder, sequined mini dress from the closet and a pair of Rene Caovilla crystal embellished wrap platform heels. My parents were going to have to accept the party dress at dinner because I wanted to step tonight.

It took me three hours to get dressed, apply a natural beat, and make it to my parents' house. Jazz music serenaded the entire house as my parents danced in the middle of the floor. My mom's glossy eyes told me that she was sipping on something good and I couldn't wait to taste test it. At our last New Year's Eve dinner, she had a ten thousand dollar bottle of Cristol that made me feel like a real rich bitch, one that spent her own money instead of her parents.

Smiling at my parents, I watched in adoration with a cheesy grin. The relationship my parents shared was something that I aspired to experience one day. They were so lovey dovey that sometimes it made me want to vomit. My dad gripped my mom's ass and I didn't want to witness shit else. Clicking my heels towards the bathroom I ran into Banks in the hallway. He was no longer in his pajamas and was wearing a pair of black slacks with a black and grey Versace sweater.

"I see you decided to get out of your pajamas for dinner," I noted.

"Yeah, you know mama would've been in this bitch crying. Hollin' 'bout Ion take shit seriously if I would've showed up how I wanted to."

I heard the running water in the bathroom behind him turn off and I leaned over to see who was in the bathroom with him. There was a pretty dark skinned woman with her natural hair flowing down her back dressed in a Versace shirt that matched Banks and a pair of leggings. My eyes darted between the two but I didn't have shit to say. It was crazy to me that Banks brought countless hoes home and got away with it.

"Zalana, this is Shadae... Shadae, this is my lil sister, Zalana."

"Hello, it's nice to meet you," she smiled so I returned the greeting before walking past them into the bathroom to wash my hands.

By the time I walked down the hallway my parents were conversing with Shadae. When I joined the party we relocated to the dining room and I wasted no time accepting a glass of the Cristol that my mom was sipping on. Pamela, my parents' personal chef, brought out the Caesar salad and we began eating. My father was a federal prosecutor turned criminal defense attorney and my mother was a stay at home mom. The life my father always provided for us was definitely one of luxury.

Growing up, we had a housekeeper come out twice a month to deep clean the house and my mother wasn't much of a cook so Pamela was on the payroll for as long as I could remember. I don't know what my parents were going to do when Ms. Pamela goes on maternity leave in a few months because I wasn't attending any family dinners if my mom cooked the food. My mom even had a stylist and I'm sure that's who picked out that nice ass color block long sleeve dress she was wearing. The manicurist and hairstylist that my mom had on the payroll were also around for years but I didn't know any of them as well as I knew Ms. Pamela because she was around the house five days of the week.

"Zalana, Banks tells us that Shadae is a middle school teacher. I was thinking that you should shadow her to see if you'd be interested in entering the education field," my father suggested before shoveling a spoonful of romaine lettuce into his mouth.

Fighting the urge to roll my eyes, I quickly replied. "Not interested. I know I don't want to be in the school system. I don't even like kids so I'll really get out here and embarrass y'all."

"I'm sorry, that wasn't a request, it was a demand," my father paused and placed his fork down on the table. "In 2022, you are going to figure your shit out. All you do is post yourself spending up all of our money on the internet. I mean at least some of these girls are smart enough to make money off of the shit. Meanwhile my daughter just does it for fun, posting your ass up on Instagram for free."

"I thought I blocked you across all of my social media platforms?" I wondered aloud.

"That doesn't mean I don't hear about the shit and that's beside the point. It's about time that you grow up and get your life together."

"Don't make it seem like I never tried. After the doctor made it clear that going back out on tour would risk the functioning in my ankle for the rest of my life, I asked to enroll in a performing arts school and you guys said no. When I said I wanted to open a dance studio, you guys said no. Banks got to live out his dream and open a nightclub that failed then you guys gave him money for his dispensary without a second thought…"

"Please don't bring me in this," Banks pleaded and I rolled my eyes at his ass.

"Why not? It seems fitting since they want to make me out to be some bum that doesn't do shit while you're fondling your pick of the month underneath the table." My revelation forced Shadae's eyes to widen as Banks repositioned his hands from between her legs under the table. I refocused my attention on my father before I continued. "Yeah but y'all are worried about me and my IG, at least I don't disrespect our family home, I don't get it. Also, I can't make money off of my social media because my accounts are all private at *your* request, daddy. Do you not remember the many lectures about internet safety because of the business you are in and my status as a single woman?"

"I do," he nodded.

"Zalana, you are a lady and you can't do the things that Banks does."

At my wits' end, I glared at Banks and Shadae as they silently observed the debate. "I'm about to take it there so she gotta get the fuck out!" Shadae looked at Banks but he knew I meant business.

"Shadae, let me walk you to the door. I'll call you when I finish up here."

She nodded her head and Banks ushered her out of the room without another word. Once I heard the front door shut behind them, I continued. "Y'all gave him the money for a whole nightclub that got shut down and he almost wound up in prison because he was selling more blow than Scarface and grandpa out of there. Daddy got him off on the charges and then he was able to go on and open a dispensary without half of the scrutiny I get."

"The difference between you and Banks is he has a business degree and came to me with a business plan for the nightclub. He put forth efforts and we gave him the money. If you did the same, we would give you the same amount of money."

"Okay, I'll work on my business plan and have a presentation prepared for you next week," I confirmed with a jovial expression as I sipped from the champagne flute. That hopeful moment was short lived because my father's next words made me feel like he just wanted to play in my face.

"No, you misunderstood. You need to obtain a degree in business first."

"Maaaaaaa," I whined as Banks re-entered the dining room. "Come on and help me out a little, we have discussed this topic a million times and you're sitting here on mute. I am you and you are me. You lived off of grandpa's money until you met daddy. No shade but you don't work and you don't have a degree or any of that so why am I catching so much slack?"

"Your father is the head of *this* family, Zalana, so everything goes through him. Go to college, obtain that degree then come back with your business plan," she slurred. Her ass was drunk and clearly not going to be any help.

"Come on y'all, we are supposed to be enjoying dinner as a family and y'all turning it into a debate," Banks expressed, walking over to rub my shoulder.

"I'm not turning dinner into anything because I'm leaving. Time and time again, I'm shown how little I mean to this family! They want to dictate my life and I'm not going for that!" I exclaimed through a fit of tears.

"Come on Zalana..." Banks attempted to console me with a hug but I shoved his ass away.

"No! You didn't have my back either. Too busy worrying about a new piece of pussy!"

Storming out of the house at full speed, I was happy as fuck that I wore my flats to dinner and planned to change into my heels afterwards because I needed to get away from my family. Tonight, I was going to King's to drink up all the free liquor and show my ass so Yola's husband could put me in rotation. It was clear that I'd never receive the same treatment as Banks and I needed to accept the facts.

CHAPTER FIVE

Benjamin "Banks" Moore

I felt like shit for not having Zalana's back. The truth was I'd been trying to get between Shadae's legs for a few months now. When I met Shadae, she was honest and told me that she had a nigga but he was in prison. I still finessed the number under the guise of *we could be friends*. Now that the nigga finally got out and she broke up with his ass, we could move forward. I tried to fuck her in my parents' bathroom as soon as we got here but she wasn't on that. The best I could do was rub that pussy through her leggings beneath the table and she let me so I wasn't even listening to shit being discussed over dinner until Zalana called my name.

This argument between Zalana and my parents wasn't shit new. They would go for a year or so and then the conversation would pop up again. Zalana would leave in tears like she just did, they would go a few months without speaking, then they'd be back like ain't shit happen. I love my baby sis and I understood where she was coming from. Our parents did hold her to a much higher standard than they did me. As Zalana vehemently explained during the argument, I had a past that involved some wild fuck ups but I was reformed now.

Art imitated life and I just knew I was going to be the next Ghost. He made selling coke out of his club seem lucrative and seamless. I mean, it was all of those things for two years then the next thing I knew, the DEA was kicking down the door and arresting me and my entire staff since they were in on the scheme. Pops made the charges disappear and I spent every penny to my name paying off my employees in exchange for their silence. When I was at my lowest, I was expecting my parents to cut me off and leave me to figure my shit out but they didn't. In fact, my father told me that I was dumb as fuck for selling illegal drugs when he could put me in the position to sell legal drugs. That next day, he paired me with a consultant to guide me through the process of opening my first dispensary that he paid the entire tab on.

Banks' Kush Depot was my pride and joy. I started this shit trying to get back in my father's good graces but it worked out for me. My Instagram bio contained the same two words since I joined the social media app *weed connoisseur.* I used to think I was an expert but when I jumped into this shit, I realized that there was so much to explore in the weed industry. All of my life, I thought I wanted to own a night-club but when I opened my dispensary, I realized that I found my true calling because the shit never felt like work. I loved handling my business and it was an indescribable feeling to know that you found your true calling.

This dance studio idea was something that Zalana talked about since we were little kids. During high school she was the captain of the dance team and my sister could hang with the best of them. Right before our high school graduation Zalana had a dance video that went viral on Youtube and she had the opportunity to tour with Beyonce straight out of high school and she took the opportunity. My parents hated that decision so they cut her off while she was out on tour. Back-ground dancers didn't make that much damn money and Zalana was accustomed to living a certain type of lifestyle so she ran through her cash quickly. Eventually, our parents had no choice but to turn that faucet back on because Zalana injured her ankle and had to take a step back from dancing or risk permanent injury. Zalana's ankle was never the same again and she was unable to return to her first love, dancing.

"Hol' up sis," I rushed out of the house behind her.

"Fuck you Banks, I don't want to talk!" Zalana sobbed, opening the door to her Benz before she slid inside. A part of me wanted to let her cry baby ass go home and cry because my parents' personal chef whipped up steak, lobster, and garlic mashed potatoes. That was my shit and I was missing out because Zalana and my parents wanted to continue this never ending argument.

"Chill baby girl, you know I always have your back," I affirmed, stopping Zalana from closing her door.

With my forearm on the hood I leaned inside of this lil ass car. "Zalana, they only have so much power over you because you allow them to feed you and..."

"You aren't any different, they fed you too!" Zalana's mad ass cut me off. Her ass was fuming, chest heaving up and down like she wanted to fight me, and all I was trying to do was spit some real shit in her ear real quick.

"Sis, I swear I get where you're coming from. We've discussed this on multiple occasions, you know I understand your frustration. It's fucked up that they wanna do you like this but that's what they are doing and that's that. Get out here and get a job or something to save up some money to do it on your own. Or else yo ass don't have a choice but to go to school and do as them old motha fuckas say."

"Yeah, you're right," she wiped her eyes. "Now my makeup is all fucked up and I was supposed to go out tonight!"

"Well take yo ass home, rest up, and we can figure some shit out in the morning. I love you," I leaned in and tried to kiss her cheek but she dodged that shit.

"We are too old for that. Ion know where yo lips be," she cringed. "I love you though. I'm going to get out of here. I know yo ass wanna go back in there and eat so enjoy."

I let her have that because my hungry ass did want to eat. Standing at a tall six feet and ten inches and weighing two hundred and ninety pounds, on my mama, a nigga wasn't missing no meals. "I will," I laughed, rubbing my stomach through my Versace Sweater.

Closing the door to Zalana's Benz, I knew I had to speak with my accountant as soon as the holidays were over. If my parents wanted to ignore Zalana's dreams I was going to step in and make them happen. Retreating to the dining room, my mother was gone and my father was seated at the table with Ms. Pamela, eating the food in silence. My father informed me that my mother went to shower because she lost her appetite. I asked Pamela to prepare two to go plates for me and she stood to exit the dining room with a silent head nod.

"Why do you guys treat Zalana like that? If she wants to open a dance studio, let her. College isn't for everyone and she doesn't just sit on her ass doing nothing. She helps me with my business."

"And we pay her a lovely salary just to work that menial position."

"I'm just saying, it's fucked up all the shit y'all did for me and the lack of efforts y'all give her."

"Slow yo roll Banks, the manner in which I choose to parent my daughter is my business. Stay in a child's place," he grilled me.

Waving his grumpy ass off, I went back to the kitchen to check the status of my to go plates. Pamela had them wrapped up and placed in a brown paper bag when I returned. With the food in hand, I went to find my mother to tell her good night and found her asleep in their bed. That champagne did her ass in tonight.

Seated inside of my GMC Denali, I turned the heat on low and placed a call to Shadae. I knew Shadae was probably going to be pissed after getting rid of her nigga yesterday then coming to dinner with me and Zalana blowing up my spot by calling her my pick of the month and kicking her out of dinner. There was some truth to Zalana's words, I always had a new bitch on my arms but Shadae didn't have to be privy to that. I been working her ass for too long to not explore the pussy now.

"What do you want, Banks?" Shadae answered the phone all dry and shit.

"Damn, I got our food to go, I'm trying to slide through."

"Hell no, you think I didn't catch your sister call me your pick of the month? You made it seem like you wanted something more than a sexual relationship but now I feel like that's not the case and I'm not on that type of time. If you a fuck boy just say that!"

Closing my eyes, I planned to get in Zalana's ass for that comment because she was about to cost me some of that good payback pussy. After all of the time I put in with Shadae, that wasn't an option. Tuning back in to Shadae's conversation I realized that her ass was lowkey snapping on me and I wasn't the nigga for that. Her ass was becoming more of a headache than I bargained for.

"You must've read the wrong nigga's name when you answered the phone. We'll try this shit again when you remember who the fuck you talking to. You know Ion play that yelling shit, you gotta communicate like an adult with me, shorty."

Disconnecting the call, I pulled out of my parents' driveway. Shadae had until the morning to call me back with a better attitude or I'd be onto the next bitch. I headed to my homeboy Rue's house where he was pre-gaming with Zaire. The entire city was going to be out bringing in the New Year and I planned to bring it in with Shadae but her attitude ruined that shit. Knocking lightly, Zaire opened the door, confused to see me.

"Wassup bih. I thought you was gone be laid up with that teacher bitch tonight?"

"Change of plans. I'm gone slide through King's with y'all," I confirmed, pulling a sac of weed out of my pocket.

"Rue in there arguing with Cici," Zaire shook his head.

Entering the home, I felt like I was in the middle of another warzone as they bickered coming down the hallway. "I ain't in here arguing with her crazy ass. She finna sit the fuck down and act like we got a pair of twins."

"Nah nigga, if you hangin' I'm swangin'. You got me fucked up if you think I'm staying here with these kids while y'all are in the streets showing y'all asses. Either we slidin' together or you ain't fuckin' going," Cici folded her arms across her chest.

"Man move, we going in the mancave cry baby ass girl."

Rue roughly kissed Cici and I brushed past them. I ain't want that shit rubbing off on me. Growing up, I watched my parents bicker and argue enough to last a lifetime. I would say that their relationship evolved over the years and they seemed to be a united front now. However, I didn't do that arguing and yelling shit with anybody outside of my family, I definitely wasn't going to do it with my shawty.

Sitting in Rue's man cave, we put ESPN on the tv while I finished rolling my blunt. I took a few pulls from the blunt then passed the blunt to Zaire. Melting into the nice ass gamer chairs that Rue had in his man cave, I needed to find out where he got these from because I wanted to put one in my crib. About twenty minutes later Rue entered the room with a bottle of Hennessy in his hand and a lit blunt dangling from his lips. Me and Zaire glanced at him once the door opened and then refocused on the game of *Madden* we were engrossed in.

"And don't be lighting blunts before you get in the mancave, act like we got a pair of twins in here," Cici mocked him before slamming the door.

"Ignore her, she on her period and shit," he shook his head.

"Whatchu doing over here? I thought you was kickin' it with that new chick?"

"My parents and Zalana got to arguing which led to my sister telling Shadae that she was the pick of the month."

"Zalana has always been a hater," Rue laughed.

"Ya feel me, cockblocking since we were teens," I joked.

My phone vibrated in my pocket and I paused the game to see who it was. With a cocky grin on my face, I hit the button to answer the call. "Yoooo."

"I'm sorry for yelling but you said you were ready and that you wanted to bring me to the dinner to show me you were ready for more."

"Do you wanna come through my spot and have dinner to bring in the New Year on my dick or not? Let me show you how ready I am."

"You lucky I've never had food prepared by a personal chef before," she sucked her teeth.

"I'm going to drop you my address. Meet me there."

"Okay."

Ending the call, I shot off the text message and tossed Rue the PS5 controller.

"I'm about to slide," I announced.

"Damn, we thought you was about to slide with us?"

"Change of plans."

"Well shit, come on Zaire, Cici hopped her ass in the shower, we need to sneak out now."

"Sayless."

Our grown asses snuck out of the house and I shook my head while

35

pulling out of the driveway. Cici was going to fuck Rue up when he came back home later. My crib was ten minutes from Rue's residence, providing me with a ten or fifteen minute buffer to shower before Shadae showed up. As I stepped out of the shower my phone alerted me that someone was on my doorstep. Wrapping a towel around my waist I slipped my feet into my house shoes and approached the front door.

Shadae's plump lips spread into a grin at the sight of me before she closed her eyes like she had to refocus her attention. If all that shit she was saying about staying loyal to her nigga until he got out of jail and nothing happening between them since he came home was true, I knew she was feening for some dick and I had enough to go around. I guess Shadae must've hit a bar or something because my nostrils detected liquor on her breath. Leaning in, I planted a kiss on her clavicle bone then up to her neck before pulling her into me. Shadae was probably mesmerized by the scent of the body wash I used. Ion even know what type of body wash it was because I stole it from Zalana's house. I spent the night over there once and used the shit she had in her guest bedroom and I'd been swiping her shit since then.

"See you trying to play hard to get," I pecked her cheek then closed and locked the front door.

"I'm not, I just..." I scooped Shadae off of her feet and carried her light ass over to the couch.

Shadae was slim and dark skinned, just how I loved my women. Although she had a small set of titties, the hips and ass made up for that. She had on an oversized sleep shirt and a pair of biker shorts to match. Sitting down with her in my lap, I kissed her gently while gliding my hands into her biker shorts. My middle and index finger felt her gushy insides and she moaned into my mouth. As wet as she was my dick rocked up instantly.

I'd been waiting to knock Shadae down for too long. Tugging at her biker shorts, Shadae lifted up to help me out. Pulling my mouth away from hers, I slid Shadae down my dick and watched her face tense up.

"You gotta relax, Shadae," I encouraged her but she was still tense as fuck.

Fighting my annoyance, I pulled out her titties and sucked one into my mouth while trying to guide her up and down my dick. I knew my shit was big but at her grown age, she should've known how to take dick. That did the trick because Shadae finally relaxed and I fucked her lil ass all over my couch. By the end of the night Shadae sucked my dick and that's when I realized that I could definitely keep her lil ass around. Laying back on the couch with Shadae on top of my chest, I felt my stomach rumbling because I never ate dinner.

"Come on, let's go eat dinner," I coerced but her ass didn't move.

Realizing that Shadae was asleep, I gently peeled her off my chest and let her sleep while I showered again and sat down to eat. It was nearing one o'clock in the morning so I could see why her ass was tired. A marathon of fucking always left bitches in a coma. I only got one forkful of steak into my mouth before a call from my homeboy Rue came in.

"Yooooo," I answered the phone, curious as fuck about what he could want this late at night.

"Wassup bih, where ya at?"

"I'm at the crib. Why? What's up?"

"Your sister down here in King's drunk as fuck," he informed me. "I was about to tell you to come get her but if it's cool with you, we will take her home since we about to slide to the after hours spot."

"Yeah man, bring her ass home. I'll be here to get her out of the whip when you pull up."

"Bet."

Disconnecting the call, I shook my head because Zalana just ruined my appetite. Behind fucking, stuffing my face with food was my next favorite thing to do so that meant I was hot. Zalana knew we didn't play that shit, her being drunk and going to the clubs was out of pocket. Especially when I knew she was down there by herself because her ass ain't have no fucking friends. My phone rang again and it was Rue calling so I knew Zalana was about to piss me off.

"Wassup?"

"Man she acting a fool and she's with that nigga Dro King's wife so I can't just snatch her up like I want to. I'm about to put her on the phone so you can rap with her," Rue yelled into the phone over the loud music.

Shadae's head popped up on the couch and the distinct sound of gagging before she ran over to my trash can to vomit only further pissed me off.

"Do you have any water? I think I had too much to drink," Shadae questioned as I passed her a napkin to clean herself up.

After passing Shadae the water, she opened it to take a swig and instantly vomited again. This year was starting out real shitty. Caring for two drunk women wasn't how I planned to spend my night. All of the feelings I'd grown for Shadae went out of the window because this was my second encounter with her drunken behavior and there wouldn't be a third time.

CHAPTER SIX

Zalana

*T**hot Shit*** by Megan Thee Stallion blared through the club and a bitch was lit. After the shit show my family called a New Year's Eve dinner, I was prepared to hit the club and have a good time. Since I didn't eat dinner before arriving, I'd be honest and say that the liquor was drinking my ass at this point and I was feeling lovely. The vibe with the ladies in Yola's section was right and I felt like I could breathe and put my family issues to the back of my mind.

I could get used to making money in the club. Standing on top of the couch rapping the chorus to the song, I knew I was drunk off my ass because my family drove me to this point. Yola and the ladies in her section welcomed me with open arms and all of the free liquor my heart desired. Shaking my ass to the beat I heard the ladies hyping me up so I went harder. I had the type of body that bitches paid for and knew how to move that shit.

"Fuck it up bitch! Fuck it up!" I heard Yola shouting before passing me another shot of liquor. My cheery ass saw Rue walking in my direction and immediately rolled my eyes. If he was here that means Banks probably wasn't far behind and my suspicions were confirmed when he interrupted the show I was putting on and leaned down to whisper in my ear.

"Sis, you at yo limits and Banks wants us to make sure you get home safely. We about to slide," Rue explained, reaching for my hand.

"No nigga! Banks ain't my daddy and I'm going to get home safely," I refuted, swatting his hand away.

"Yeah, she's straight. Me and my husband are going to make sure she gets home safely," Yola cut in.

The music changed to *Back In Blood* by Pooh Shiesty and I got into character rapping along to the beat as Rue stepped off. Unfortunately, the nigga was right back in my face moments later shoving his phone up against my ear.

"Aye Zalana, I'm only going to say this once. Get yo ass in the car with Rue," Banks exclaimed.

"Banks, you're not my fucking daddy and you didn't even have my back at dinner like my big brother should have," I slurred into the phone, realizing that I should switch to drinking water for the rest of the evening.

"I told you she is going to be alright, I'm going to make sure she gets home," Yola yelled at Rue.

"Zalana! If I have to say it again, I'm going to come down there and embarrass yo ass. You know I don't like you going to hang out like that unless I'm in the club and you know I'll embarrass that ass!"

Stomping my feet, I turned to Yola to hug her and tell her good-night. With my arms folded across my chest, I trailed Rue and Banks' other friend Zaire out of the club. Rue had the phone to his ear for another thirty seconds before sliding it back into his pocket. "What about my car?" I challenged him once we stepped outside. Now that the temperature dropped even further, I wished I wore something more fitting for the weather instead of trying to be cute.

"Yo ass ain't driving home in your condition," Rue shot back.

"I hope you didn't park far," rubbing my hands up and down my arms trying to remain warm.

"Nah, we around the back. Maybe next time you'll wear something weather appropriate instead of trying to be cute. It's been about sixty degrees all damn day so I know yo ass was cold when you got here, don't complain now."

"Fuck you Rue," I hiccuped.

"Nah, Ion get down like that with my homie's sisters. A cousin maybe, but not a sister. Plus you clearly don't hold your liquor well."

"Whatever," I grumbled.

When we got inside of the truck I sat silently for the duration of the ride. Banks had one thing right, I needed to stop letting everybody feed me because they felt like they could run my life. All I wanted to do was open my dance studio but nobody wanted to see me happy. At least that's what the liquor was telling my drunk ass. Not ready to go home for real, I requested an Uber to meet me in front of my house. It was five minutes away so it should've arrived around the same time as us. Once I verified that I should be looking for an older black gentleman driving a black Toyota Corolla, I relaxed in the seat and slid my phone back into my purse.

Approaching my townhouse, I rolled my eyes because the Uber wasn't parked in front of my house but two doors down. This was going to force me to run to the car because I already saw Rue initiating a call to Banks. His bossy ass was about to try and play like he was my daddy but I wasn't having it. Once Rue stopped the car I hopped out and ran down the block towards the black Toyota Corolla. The throbbing in my ankle told me that this was a horrible idea but I kept going anyway, like I said before, the liquor was in control.

"Zalana!" Banks shouted behind me but I didn't let up until I was seated in the back of the car.

"Come on drive! I know you see that nigga rushing towards the car!"

As directed, my Uber driver mashed the gas and sped down Davis Boulevard until we were on Adalia Avenue. My phone pinged and I pulled it out of my purse. There was a message on the screen from the Uber app saying that my driver had arrived. Squinting at the screen, I saw a message from the Uber driver come through the app.

Uber Driver: I am outside of the address provided but I was approached by a group of men and told to leave. I circled the block just in case you would like to walk to meet me somewhere else.

After reading that message I realized that I misread the description of the car earlier. I should've been waiting for a Toyota Camry and not a Corolla. Glancing up at the driver, I noticed he wasn't an older black man but probably was more my age, if not younger, and the car was lacking an Uber sticker or decal.

"Hey, ummmm, I think I am just going to walk. You can let me out here and I'll pay you cash," I muttered. He nodded his head and the car came to a stop. Reaching for the door handle I pulled it but there was clearly a child lock on. Before I had a chance to further process the severity of the situation, another car pulled alongside us and my door was ripped open.

"Help!" I screamed as two masked men pulled me from the backseat. Kicking and screaming, I put up a good fight but I was no match for two men. Once they had a hold on me, my mouth was duct taped and I was shoved into the backseat of the car. The man who I thought was the Uber driver sat in the backseat with a gun in his hand.

"Get the fuck in the car and relax. If you can follow directions and chill the fuck out, you'll make it out of this alive. If not, it won't take shit to give you one to the back of the head."

The murderous scowl he wore was a clear signal that he meant every word he grumbled. Sobbing quietly, I did as I was ordered, regret sweeping through me. I should've taken my ass home like Banks said, now I was in the hands of some devious mother fuckers. The two men outside of the car moved around and I watched through the window until they lit the Corolla on fire and jumped in the front seat of the car we were seated in and sped off.

CHAPTER SEVEN

Streetz

This might sound fucked up but I felt like a weight was lifted off of my shoulders when that text came through on Shadae's phone. Although the shit that happened last year with her and the abortion killed me and diminished the love I had for her, I still felt like I needed her. Now that I didn't have Shadae, it was just me now and I needed to pull that trigger. Dressed in a pair of basketball shorts and a black t-shirt I grabbed from the corner store this morning, I was prepared to hit the block and bring in the New Year shooting dice and playing cards. I might have enjoyed my space, but I was making an exception tonight because I loved to take a nigga's money.

When I pulled up to Cheese's spot not too far from the trap house that I was staying in until I found a legit spot, the loud ass music almost made me want to turn around but I needed to do something to keep my mind off of my personal life.

"Hey, Streetz," some bitch greeted me when I stepped out of my black 1967 Chevy Impala. Offering a slight head nod without glancing her way, I had tunnel vision, scanning my surroundings before approaching the front door.

"That nigga so mean but so mufuckin' fine," I heard the girl trying to whisper to her friend but my antennas were always up for motha fuckas whispering.

Ignoring them, I made sure that I recognized all four cars lined up along the curb before I continued into the house. As Cheese promised, it was just him and two other niggas I was cool with, Marvin and Will, in here shooting dice.

"Oh you brought this silent nigga out here to play huh?" Marvin noted before dapping me up.

I silently returned the gesture and did the same with Will while they talked shit.

"Fuckin' right, we about to sit down and play spade since my nigga stopped through."

"This nigga only called you because I'm already up fo' bands on his bitch ass," Will noted.

Nodding my head, I sat down at the table and watched as Cheese shuffled and dealt the cards. "We glad to see you home baby," Marvin stated picking up his cards.

"Definitely," I monotoned, scanning my hand.

"But what really brought you over here? You never slide through for shit like this so wassup?" Cheese quizzed.

"You wanna talk like a hoe or play cards?" I grilled him as Marvin tossed out the first card, a king of diamonds.

"We finna play nigga," Cheese laughed. "But now I see, since you comparing me to hoes, it's something with Shadae ain't it?"

I didn't say shit, just waited for my turn and tossed out a card. You'd think that Cheese would know me well enough to know I ain't like discussing a fuckin' thing with nobody unless we were talking business. Nobody knew about the breakup, Shadae's abortion, or none of that shit. The only reason motha fuckas even knew I tried to snap Shadae's daddy's neck was because I went to prison behind that. Although I didn't have much to say, Cheese, Will, and Marvin knew that was just me and didn't take any offense to it. We'd been cool since the ninth grade so they knew this was always in my character.

Pulling out a sack of weed and a few packs of blunts, I rolled up while continuing to play the game, I wanted to bring in the New Year high as fuck. A little after two o'clock in the morning these niggas started calling bitches over and I made my exit. The last thing I wanted to do was start 2022 with some bitches all up in my face trying to talk to me and shit, I wasn't with it.

Taking the short drive back to the trap house, I had a lot of shit on my mind. After pissing and showering, I took a swig from the bottle of D'Usse sitting on the coffee table and made sure my glock had one in the chamber before laying back to scroll on Zillow. I took a moment to save a few houses for me to contact when everything opened back up on the second. I stood from the couch to head to the back bedroom where I had a lil blow up mattress.

When I opened the door, I had to close my eyes and focus to make sure that my mind wasn't playing tricks on me. A gorgeous ass Megan Thee Stallion looking chick stood in the back of the room with fear written all over her face and a sliver of duct tape covering her mouth. Her caramel skin contrasted with the black mascara running from her almond shaped eyes. She was dressed in a black dress that hugged her body tightly, displaying all the ass and titties that she possessed. I didn't know what was going on but I knew who did. Stepping back out of the room I whipped out my phone and called the niggas that used to run this trap house for me, it ain't no way these motha fuckas were that dumb.

"Yoooo," Redd answered the phone. Sounding like he took his ass over there where Cheese and the rest of them niggas were at.

"Where the fuck you at?" I gritted into the phone.

"Cheese's lil jump off spot. Why, wassup?"

"Get over to your old spot."

"Streetz, let me..."

I hung up on his ass before he could finish his statement. Redd was my Aunt Victoria's son and if this motha fucka wasn't my lil cousin, I swear I would snap this nigga's neck. If I did that, my Aunt Victoria would hate me more than she already did. When Redd came to me, begging to get put on so he could help take care of his disabled mother, I felt bad for him and caved. I was regretting that shit like a motha fucka now. Furious, I rolled another blunt to help ease my mind while I waited for this nigga to pull up.

When I saw the headlights beaming through the window I put the blunt out and waited for Redd to step inside. I was caught completely off guard when I saw Santiago and Breon barge through the front door with Redd. This nigga had my entire crew on this side of town involved in some bullshit. Slick ass motha fuckas would've gone undetected too if I didn't decide to crash here instead of grabbing a hotel room.

The only reason I decided to crash here instead of a hotel room was because Shadae still had access to my accounts until the banks reopened on the second. She was definitely the type of bitch to be watching my shit then pop up on a nigga. The way I was feeling I would throw her ass through a wall next.

"You three weak ass niggas can't get pussy so you stealing it now?" I accused before exhaling deeply.

"Nah, let me explain..."

"We only did it because of the money..."

"We not gone hurt her..."

They all spouted off at once, loud enough for the bitch in the room to hear. Aggressively waving my hand in the air, I silenced these three dumb asses without uttering a word. Pointing at Redd, I signaled for him to speak.

"We were approached by this Spanish nigga to snatch ol' girl. It wasn't supposed to go down tonight. I was supposed to snatch her on the second when Mario Lucero's trial started but I was sitting outside of her crib just watching the comings and goings because I didn't know shit about this girl then she hopped in my whip thinking I was her Uber so I seized the moment."

"Why the fuck would you be involved in some shit like this?"

"They was paying top dollar, two hundred and fifty thousand dollars, and we don't have to hurt her or anything. Just hold her until his trial is over. I guess she's related to a witness or some shit," he shrugged.

Glancing up at the ceiling, I attempted to locate a place of zen so I wouldn't fuck these lil niggas up but after taking a few breaths while they waited anxiously, I never found that place. Without warning, I lunged at them, grabbing Redd up by his throat while I knocked Breon and Santiago in their mouths. One jab from my right hand had both of their mouths leaking. Redd's face resembled a tomato as he clawed at my hands. Just when I knew he was seeing the light, I released his neck.

This was exactly why I still felt like I didn't have family, even with Redd on my team. The nigga had done some dumb shit since I put him on three years ago but this was the most asinine. "Don't shit move unless I say so! The bitch done seen my face and shit because I went in there oblivious to her presence. So now if y'all let her go, she can identify me and I ain't even have shit to do with this." Pausing for a moment, I scanned all three of their faces before speaking again. "Y'all got me talking more than I like to. Clean up all that fucking blood on my floor. Make sure the bitch has something to drink and doesn't piss on my floor. I'll figure something out by sunrise." Exiting the trap house, I went to a hotel. If Shadae decided to bring her silly ass there, I was going to handle her ass accordingly.

~

The next morning I woke up and used the hotel amenities to handle my hygiene. 2022 was already off to a bullshit ass start and it couldn't get worse than possibly going down for a kidnapping that you ain't have shit to do with. I was a meticulous ass nigga but I didn't know how I was going to get out of this shit. Usually, I was down for some *no face no case* shit but I didn't put my gun on women and children. Plus that girl ain't deserve to lose her life because Redd, Breon, and Santiago were incompetent ass holes.

Gathering the few items I brought with me to the hotel, I scanned the room twice before making my exit. On the way out of the Westin, I checked my call logs and hadn't received anything from Redd so shit better be straight when I got over there. Looking up from my phone, my eyes connected with Shadae leaned up against my whip. Taking another deep breath, I continued my stride, ready to ignore this bitch.

"Streetz, we need to talk," she proclaimed. Scooting her ass out of my path I opened my car door and her nutty ass jumped in between me and the door frame. Placing my hands on my temples, I gently massaged them before exhaling deeply. "You're not leaving until you

47

talk to me. I don't want to throw away our relationship or friendship that easily," she confessed.

"You threw our seed away that easily. You hopped on another nigga's dick that easy," I pushed her ass back by her neck, making sure I squeezed the hickey she tried to cover up. "Move around Shadae, you know Ion like to do too much talking."

Ion know what gave Shadae the courage but the bitch lunged at me, swinging her lil ass arms rapidly. She caught me in the face and I gripped that same hand she used to assault me and folded it behind her back. Shadae screeched in pain but I didn't give a fuck. Scooping her ass up off of the ground, I paused for a moment and caught myself, remembering that she was a female just before I dropped her on her head. Standing still for a moment, I slammed her on the car parked next to mine. Shadae scooted across the hood and away from me, knowing her ass fucked up and I wasn't up for her bullshit.

Nah, I wasn't the type to put my hands on a female but I'd yoke her ass up to keep her up off of me. Bringing the engine to life, I rolled down the window and glared at Shadae who was still peering at me. "I'll send somebody to pick up my other car on Monday and you better not touch my shit." Swerving out of the parking spot, Shadae jumped back to make sure I didn't hit her ass. We should've never taken our friendship to the romantic lane and maybe then I'd still have my best friend.

Unfortunately, this bitch standing in front of me wasn't the girl I used to know. Something about her was different, I couldn't put my finger on it and I didn't give a fuck to do so either. When I'd brought it up in the past she would say having an abortion changed a lot of women but I didn't believe that was it, it was something else. At the end of the day, it was the next nigga's problem and not mine.

CHAPTER EIGHT

Banks

*A*fter Zalana ran off I received a text from her saying she was taking an Uber to a hotel so she could have her space. If space was what she wanted, I was going to let her ass have it. I still checked her location to make sure that's actually where she was going while I stood around with the fellas smoking a blunt.

When I finally did head back inside I called one of Shadae's cousins to come pick her drunk ass up. She was mad as fuck but I needed to chop it up with my niggas since they were here. If I wasn't taking care of Zalana then I wasn't taking care of Shadae either. Plus something just didn't sit right with me about her, the bitch acted so high class like she had her shit together but I couldn't get with the constant need for validation. Putting a title on things when she just ended a relationship and ending a relationship and jumping right into this shit didn't sit right with me after chopping it up with my bros. Add in Shadae's inability to control her liquor and it was a fuckin' wrap.

We threw back a few shots to celebrate the New Year before they left as well and I got into my bed solo, just how I loved it. When I woke up this morning the first thing I did was shoot my accountant an email, instructing her to see how much money I could gift Zalana without hurting my own pockets. If my baby sis wanted to open a dance studio then I was going to make sure that shit happened for her. After getting that straight, I adjusted my employees' schedules for the next two weeks. I wanted to make sure that Zalana had as much time off as she needed to start working on her own dreams.

With business out of the way, I went to my gym on the fourth floor and worked out for a good thirty minutes before I received a phone call from my mom. "Happy New Year, ma. I tried to tell you that before I left last night but you were knocked out."

"Yeah, that champagne really did a number on me," she explained before hiccuping in my ear.

"I know you not drinking this early in the morning?" I queried.

"Just a few mimosas, nothing too heavy," she replied. I shook my head because if she wasn't sipping wine, she was out drinking mimosas. This wasn't anything new, I was used to my mother sipping on her wine and shit since we were kids but now it seemed to be more frequent and her behavior was affected because of it. "Have you spoken with Zalana today? Her location is off and we were supposed to go to brunch this morning but she isn't answering."

"That crazy girl left here in an Uber to go to a hotel last night. She said she needed space."

"You let your sister get into an Uber, Banks?" My mother gasped and I knew she was going to start the dramatics. "Ezra!"

"What Zenobia?" I heard my father question in the background.

"I told you how Zalana turned her location off and isn't answering the phone. Well Banks said Zalana left in an Uber last night because she needed space. I have a bad feeling about this. Zalana has never turned her location off before. No matter how mad she is."

"Put your phone on speaker and let me speak with Banks," he urged before taking over the phone call. "Do you know what hotel she went to Banks? I'm just going to check on her."

"Ummmm, I checked last night and she was at the Country Inn & Suites off of Dale Mabry."

"The Country Inn & Suites?" My mom wheezed. "No, take me there right now! I need to lay eyes on my child. She would *never* stay in a Country Inn & Suites! Let me check her credit card, that's what I should've done first."

If I didn't know my sister this would've been some funny shit but her boujie ass wouldn't have stayed in a Country Inn & Suites. She always told me not to book a hotel room for her if the property didn't have a full restaurant and spa on site.

"Are you sure that's the hotel, Banks?"

"I'm positive, ma," I expressed, climbing off of the treadmill to locate my phone since I answered through my Airpods. Without uttering a word to my folks, I attempted to call Zalana on the other line but it went straight to her voicemail. Clicking back over, I heard my mom in a full panic saying that Zalana didn't pay for any hotel rooms on her credit cards last night.

"Zenobia, sit yo ass down. Yo ass been drinking those lil champagne drinks since you got up this morning and you are starting to piss me off. Let us figure out what's going on," my dad commanded. I was happy that he said exactly what I was thinking because she was doing too much. My phone pinged in my ear and I pulled it away from my face to check my notifications.

"Hol' up, Zalana just sent me a voice clip. Let me listen then I'm going to call you right back," I notified them before disconnecting the call. Opening the voice clip I listened to Zalana's voice.

"Hey, Banks, I'm staying at the Country Inn & Suites and I'll be home on Monday. Sorry I ran off like that last night, I just want my space for a lil. I love you so much. I know that I don't always act like it but I appreciate you, mom, and daddy. Tell them that I love them too."

Initially, Zalana sounded like her ass was just as tipsy as her mama right now. Listening further it could've been that she was hungover after the way she behaved last night. A part of me felt like I should've gone after her ass last night but another part of me felt like she really needed the space that she insisted on having. If the girl wanted space I would make sure she had it until Monday.

Me: Okay sis. I love you. Call me if you need anything. When you come home we are going to discuss your dance studio and what we need to do to get it off of the ground.

Zalana: I love you too.

Shaking my head, I called my pops' phone to get him to control his wife because Zalana was fine and I had plans to start the New Year in Key West with my niggas and a few pretty hoes so that's where I was headed.

CHAPTER NINE

Zalana

*E*xcruciating pain shot through my feet while I stood in the corner of the room. My persistent cries fell on deaf ears because they were muffled by the duct tape covering my mouth. I spent the entire night standing in the corner, dressed in my heels while holding my bladder. At any moment I was going to piss on myself and nobody came in here since they made me send my brother that bullshit ass voice clip yesterday morning. I wanted to show my ass and refuse to recite the lines they prepared for me but the big ass gun nuzzled against my temple forced me into submission.

On the average day, I hated when people referred to me as boujie, especially my family because I was truly a product of my environment and got the shit from my mama. Yesterday I was praying that Banks would inform my mother of my whereabouts when I didn't show up for our brunch date and she would know something was wrong. The last hotel I would be caught dead frequenting was a Country Inn & Suites. If the hotel didn't have a full restaurant and spa on site then it wasn't my speed. Time continued to dwindle and I hadn't heard my phone ring yet. The men forced me to give them my passcode so they would know if my brother called or texted back with questions but I hadn't heard anything but a chime immediately after they sent the voice memo.

Sleep deprived with a full bladder, I waddled past the air mattress on the floor and over to the bedroom door. They told me I could sleep on it but I refused, the shit looked dreadful. I could only imagine how many people slept on it before I arrived here. Plus I witnessed the men who were holding me captive trek right across the bed in the same shoes they wore outside. There was no way that I could lay on that filthy thing. My sensitive skin wouldn't allow it.

Upon reaching the bedroom door, I used my bound hands to tap on the door. I made sure it was loud enough for my captors to hear me without sounding aggressive. The door swung open and a man with a ski mask concealing his identity stood there with a gun in his hand. Speaking through the duct tape only emitted low muffles. He stepped closer to me and snatched the duct tape off of my mouth.

"I really really need to use the bathroom," I expressed.

He stood in front of me and tittered his head from side to side while he looked up at the ceiling as if he was thinking. I didn't know what was so difficult about the request, I had to piss but I had to keep my shit together because that gun gave him the upperhand. Standing at five feet and ten inches, I would've definitely taken my chances to fight his ass because he was about my height and scrawny as fuck. Me, on the other hand, I was a thick one hundred and seventy pound collard greens and cornbread fed bitch so I had him on the weight for sure. Plus I worked out regularly and wasn't weak by a long shot. While my thoughts ran rampant I guess he finally made a decision.

"Go handle your business and don't try no funny shit. The window is boarded up and the only thing in there is toilet paper and soap so don't waste your time looking for a weapon or no shit like that," he commanded.

Tucking his gun on his waist, he whipped out a pocket knife and cut me from the duct tape that bound my wrists, instantly restoring a sense of freedom. The bathroom was to the left of us and I turned to walk that way as he slid the knife into his pocket. My ears were listening intently and I didn't hear anybody else in the house besides us. With my hands free, I felt a duty to at least attempt to save my own life because I still didn't know what these men wanted from me. The fact that they forced me to send my brother a voice clip that said I needed space instead of asking for money didn't sit right in my spirit. I'd rather die fighting than become a nigga's sex slave.

Closing my eyes as I approached the bathroom door, I immediately changed courses and charged at the man in the ski mask. Utilizing every source of power in my body, I knocked his ass in the head and we were both going for the gun he tucked into his waist. I flung my elbow back, attempting to hit him with it again, and his ski mask slid off. This made me fight harder because now I fucked up and caught a glimpse of his face.

WAP!

He slapped the shit out of me, proving that I underestimated his ass. Stumbling back, I felt like a cartoon character as stars floated around my head.

"What the fuck is this? Nigga, you in here putting yo hands on her? She's cu .n, Ion give a fuck what y'all was paid to do!" The man who entered the room and seemed to be shocked to see me barked, pulling the other man away from me. Since I didn't know his name I decided to refer to him as "Tall Man" because that's what he was. Eyeballing it, I could tell he was at least six feet and five inches tall, he could have a little more height on him but I couldn't say for sure without a measuring stick. He was dark skinned with a scruffy chin strap and mustache. His hair was braided straight back and neat as fuck so I knew it was fresh. While staring the Tall Man down, the scrawny nigga spoke up again.

"I was trying to let her stupid ass go to the bathroom and as soon as I cut her loose, she started fighting a nigga. You told us not to be on no pervy shit so I was trying to give her space to piss with privacy but clearly she don't deserve that shit."

"You okay?" I nodded my head up and down in confirmation. "You trying to finesse or piss?" Tall Man quizzed, his voice low and emotionless.

"I have to use the bathroom for real," I sobbed, disappointment and defeat evident in my voice.

"Don't do no dumb shit," Tall Man commanded before turning to the other man. He paused for a moment, noticing that I hadn't moved then glared back at me. "GO!" He scowled.

I swiftly shuffled my way into the bathroom, disgust filling me with each step because I was bare feet in a bathroom that wasn't my own. The front door opened and there was low chatter that I couldn't make out as I relieved my bladder and washed my hands. Approaching the door, I could make out Tall Man's voice and he was furious.

"The only reason I ain't kill you niggas and send her on her way is because she saw my face and ain't no telling what type of shit y'all would be on if I made y'all move her to another spot. He was just in here slapping her around. Make that *the last time* either one of y'all touches her. She looks like she ain't slept, did y'all even feed her?" I heard the Tall Man addressing the men.

"That bitch acting like she too good to lay on the air mattress so she been standing in the corner looking crazy and we offered her food and she looked at it like she ain't want none." I would *never* forget that chilling voice and it belonged to the one who I thought was the Uber driver. His voice sent chills down my spine and sent flashbacks of him pointing the gun at me through my mind. He definitely sounded like he was the mastermind behind my kidnapping but the man who just saved me from an asswhooping clearly struck fear in all of them. After a long deep breath, I wiped my wet hands on my dress then stepped out of the bathroom. All eyes darted in my direction and I knew I had to give in and eat something because I was dizzy now.

"May I please have something to eat?" I inquired, looking down at my feet. The last thing I wanted to do was look at Tall Man's face again, I wanted to make it out of whatever this bullshit was alive. The man behind my kidnapping was terrifying but even these niggas were clearly fearful of Tall Man and that left me petrified.

"One of y'all go to McDonald's for her," he barked.

"Ummm, I don't eat McDonald's," I hesitantly notified him.

"See this bitch acting like she at a fuckin' boujie ass resort or some shit... like we her fuckin' butlers." Snapping my neck in his direction, I wanted to say something but he had a gun so I remained silent.

"Shut the fuck up, take her order and get the fuck on," Tall Man demanded before walking off.

After a deep breath, the man who received the directive glared at me. "What the fuck you eat then, madam?"

"The only fast food places I eat at are PDQ and Chick-Fil-A."

"Ain't no PDQ over here and Chick-Fil-A is closed on Sunday so think of some other shit quick."

"Can you just find somewhere that has a chicken caesar salad?" I faltered.

"Yeah man," he grumbled before stalking off.

The other man re-entered the home just as he left to find me something to eat. One of the men walked over with duct tape in hand, ready to strip me of any power again. While he duct taped my hand, I literally felt myself about to break down in an emotional fit but I fought it this time. With my hands secured, the man pushed me towards the bedroom.

"Nah." Tall Man voiced before stepping into the kitchen. The other men glanced at each other, appearing just as confused as me. Watching the kitchen, I waited for Tall Man to exit and provide an explanation.

"Sit on the couch, it's new. You can sleep if you want to. As long as you don't try shit, you straight. I'mma be here," he listlessly explained.

"Go 'head," one of the other men urged with a head nod and I strutted down the hallway and into the living room.

The couch appeared to be new and I leaped at the opportunity to claim a seat. Relief spread from the balls of my feet through the tips of my toes. Until that moment I didn't realize how much my back and legs were hurting as well. Against my wishes, a deep sigh escaped my lips as I closed my eyes to revel in the relief I desperately needed. When my eyes popped open, I caught a glimpse of Tall Man swaggering in front of me. This man was so fine and if we hadn't met under these circumstances, he would definitely be my type. Bossed the fuck up without the need to do too much. While I was busy sneaking glances at his profile, he plopped down on the couch beside me with his legs wide open and powered on the television. I did my best to control my breathing when he sat next to me. My nerves were fucked up because Tall Man was fine and menacing plus this entire situation was wreaking havoc on my nerves while he was relaxed watching football.

Trying to distract my mind, I wondered what cologne he was wearing. It smelled delectable and as a lady who loved scents, I detected hints of a citrus fruit and a few other fragrances. I spent my time trying to pinpoint the other scents but my mental trick clearly wasn't doing the job because my legs shook vigorously and I couldn't control it. I know that Tall Man felt it too because he looked over at me after a few moments on the couch next to me. "Relax, ain't shit gone happen to you."

"I don't know that," I quipped.

"You smoke?"

Nodding my head yes, I prayed that he would let me smoke because I needed something to take the edge off. He slid a sac of weed out of his pocket and looked over at the men on the other side of the room. "Hand me one of them Grabba Leafs out the cabinet."

One of the men silently followed his command and I waited patiently for him to roll the blunt. I wasn't a big weed head but I usually smoked at least a blunt a day. Half when I woke up in the morning and the other half in the evening before bed to help me decompress. However, I hadn't smoked since I was in the club the other night.

When Tall Man lit the blunt he held it up to my lips to assist me. I took a long hard pull from the blunt, desperate to experience the type of high that might actually put me to sleep. As I pulled the smoke into my lungs, Tall Man watched me intently. Staring back into his eyes I could sense that he had a story and the nosey bitch in me wanted to hear it. Everything about this man was captivating and I wondered why he was associated with these buffoons.

Exhaling, I ensured that the smoke blew out of the right side of my face so it wasn't slapping Tall Man in his. "You don't have to do all of that. I love the second hand smoke too or else I would've moved out of your face," he spoke and I swallowed the lump that formed in my throat. After two additional pulls from the blunt I was no longer intimidated by his stare, the superior weed he blessed me with already had me feeling good. I wanted to go for a fourth pull but Tall Man leaned back to his side of the couch and smoked a little himself while he refocused on the football game.

Halfway through the blunt, Tall Man leaned back over and allowed me to take a few additional pulls. Now I was high as fuck and hungry as hell. On cue, the door opened and the man who went to grab food returned with a bag from Panera Bread. Begrudgingly, he sat the bag in my lap and headed back out the door.

"What, you gone feed the bitch too?" The man with the chilling voice queried before exiting the house next.

"If I feel like it, nigga," he shot back.

Tall Man stood from the couch and left the living room momentarily and returned with a small knife. He cut me out of the duct tape and reclaimed his seat on the couch. I wasted no time digging into the chicken caesar salad, devouring the ingredients until the bowl was empty.

"Do you have any water?" I hesitantly requested.

"It's in the refrigerator," he nodded his head towards the kitchen.

Standing from the couch, I sauntered into the kitchen and grabbed a bottle of water from the refrigerator before returning to the couch. As bad as I wanted to stay awake, this was hour thirty and my body was exhausted from standing in that corner for such an extended period of time. Leaning my head on the arm of the sofa, I pulled my feet onto the couch and curled up in the fetal position. I prayed that he wouldn't look at my feet because they were dirty as hell from walking around without any shoes on since they brought me to that house. As if someone flipped a switch, I dozed off as soon as I found a comfortable position.

When I woke up it was dark outside but the light from the dining room where the men were gathered provided a small amount of light. My body was covered with a blanket that carried the same scent as the Tall Man, signaling that it belonged to him and it was clean. I remained still because they were discussing me and I needed to gather all of the details that I could.

"So you really think we should let her go although she saw both of y'all faces? Do you really think that's smart?" The man with the chilling voice quizzed.

"Ion know," one of the other men added.

"With the shit you went through when you were younger, I always thought you was a cold ass nigga. If she gotta go she gotta go."

His statement stung and I listened intently because I observed the coldness in Tall Man's eyes earlier. He was fine as fuck, but I clocked those murderous eyes when the man with the chilling voice asked Tall Man was he going to feed me earlier. I also knew he had a dark life story because his eyes reminded me of my grandpa's and his history would leave the hardest man in tears. Apprehension spread throughout my body as I held my breath, waiting for his reply.

"Ion think she got a look at my face for real," the man I tussled with expressed. "As soon as she made my shit slide off, I looked away. It's really *this* nigga whose face she got a good look at."

"Wake her up and do y'all thing so we can get this shit over with," Tall Man ordered.

I kept my eyes closed and relaxed until I felt someone nudge me. "Wake up." Displaying my best acting skills, I groggily opened my eyes and stared up at the man with the chilling voice. "Sit up straight, we 'bout to record this ransom video and send it to your pops."

Slowly nodding, I sat up as directed and waited for them to start the video. The ringleader stood in front of me with his ski mask in place while another man held my phone up to record. ***"Mr. Moore, we have your daughter,"*** he spoke into a voice distorter and stepped to the side. I peered into the camera, embarrassed that the camera was capturing my disheveled appearance in 4K. ***"As you can see, we have had Zalana since New Year's Eve but we are keeping her safe. Our demands are simple, we heard you haven't been putting your best foot forward on Lucero's case. Make sure you win his case in court tomorrow, your daughter's life depends on it."***

He ended the video and walked around to observe his handiwork. Tall Man stalked over to me and dropped a bag from Walmart onto my lap and retreated to the dining room to roll a blunt. Scanning the contents of the bag, there were a few packs of panties in different sizes, a jogger set, a toothbrush, slippers, towel, rag, and Dove body wash. On the average day I didn't fuck with Dove, I used natural body wash and soaps from HoneyMilk but this would have to do for today.

"Can I go take a shower?" I directed at Tall Man.

He nodded his head, never losing focus on rolling his blunt. Glee-fully standing from the couch, I went into the bathroom and took a shower. My spirits were lifted after hearing that they weren't asking for money, they only wanted my father to win his case. If there was one thing I knew about my father, he was a beast in the courtroom and would do everything within his power to attain a not guilty verdict. When I was released, I would never mention Tall Man either because I'd overheard enough to know that he wasn't involved but accidentally came here and I saw his face. Plus, if it wasn't for him, I'm sure the other men would have treated me horribly. While scrubbing my body clean I had to pause for a moment, maybe Tall Man was only being nice to me because he didn't want me to snitch on him when this was all over. Brushing those thoughts off, I focused on handling my hygiene.

Feeling a step closer to myself again, I exited the bathroom and returned to the couch. Silently claiming my seat on the couch I noticed that Tall Man was now in the dining room smoking another blunt. The weed Tall Man had was majestic and he was nice enough to share earlier so I decided to shoot my shot.

"Can I hit the blunt?" I faltered.

Tall Man eyed me and took another pull from the blunt. His intense gaze told me he was searching my face for something but I didn't know what. Maybe deception or a conniving plan to escape but I didn't have any of that on my mind. I felt like they would let me go after this was over with. Standing from his chair, Tall Man stalked over to the couch and took a seat on the opposite side from me and passed me the blunt. I accepted it and took another long pull from the blunt. While I allowed the weed smoke to invade my lungs the front door opened again and one of the masked men stepped through the door.

"Since you clearly took a liking to the bitch and over here smoking weed, can you watch her tonight? We got shit to do."

Tall Man nodded his head and the other man exited the house as swiftly as he entered. "How they snatch you?" He interrogated me once we were alone again.

"I was tipsy and high as fuck leaving the club so I wasn't paying attention when I got into the back of the car with one of them. I thought it was my Uber," I revealed, taking another pull from the blunt. I wanted to have some alone time so fucking bad and my ass got more than I bargained for.

"Why the fuck you taking Ubers after the club anyways?"

"I wasn't. My brother's friend actually took me out of club and made me go home because all they do is fucking snitch me out to my brother. Banks acts like he's my fuckin' daddy and I didn't want to hear his mouth so I requested an Uber to meet me at my house. If I would've left the club with the girls like I planned to, none of this shit would've happened. Or if I wasn't lit and more alert, I'd be safe at home."

"Nah, don't beat yourself up. Them lil niggas were paid to do a job and they were scoping you out to execute. They were going to get you either way, you just fell into their lap easier than expected. I hope this is a lesson for you to do better. Ion wanna sound like a misogynist but women are more vulnerable than men so you can't move like that. You gotta be on yo shit and aware of your surroundings at all times because next time, it might not be these niggas snatching you up. Get a gun and learn how to shoot that bitch. Don't just buy that shit to look cute in your purse. Grab you some mace and a taser then learn how to use 'em too."

"Trust me, you don't have to tell me shit. I'm going to be a totally different woman after this ordeal because I never want to be in this situation again," I lamented and took another pull from the blunt. His advice didn't go unheard and I planned to do all of those things as soon as I got out of this situation.

"When you're leaving work, the gym, or any of the places you frequent often, switch that shit up, don't go to the same locations or travel the same route. You gotta make it difficult for a motha fucka to clock yo moves on a daily basis." I nodded and coughed a little before passing the blunt back to Tall Man. "And I'm going to be a hypocrite for saying this shit but cut down on yo weed consumption so you can be alert."

Every word he uttered came out harsh but I felt the intentions were pure and I appreciated them. We finished the blunt and Tall Man disappeared into the kitchen and returned with a bag of ice. "Here, put this on your face, your cheek is a lil read from your scuffle earlier," he ordered.

Accepting the ice, our fingers collided and I promise I felt a connection between us. These feelings had to come from the weed though, right? This had to be a trauma response. I gently placed it on my throbbing cheek and prayed the slap to the face didn't leave a mark because his kindness was already leaving a mark on my heart. I found myself asleep shortly afterwards, my body desperately needed the rest.

CHAPTER TEN

Ezra Moore

*A*fter finishing dinner with Zenobia, I went into my office and reviewed some paperwork for the case I was currently focused on. I was representing the offspring of a mafia boss by the name of Mario Lucero who was hemmed up on a murder charge. All the prosecutors had for evidence was an elderly eyewitness, a lackluster motive, and my client's phone hitting off a nearby cell phone tower. Up until this point, I felt like the case was going great. I was able to trip up and discredit the eyewitness and prove that my client's cell phone was stolen earlier that day and disabled because he thought he misplaced his phone and would eventually locate it.

Tomorrow, we were giving closing arguments and the jury would begin deliberations. While in my office, I reviewed the key points I wanted to drive home with the jury as my phone vibrated on my desk. It was a video message from Zalana, my biggest fucking headache. I didn't understand where we went wrong with her.

My own daughter provided substantial insight on the great nature versus nurture debate. Zalana grew up in the same house as Banks, was provided an identical lifestyle and opportunities, but she still felt like she didn't have to live up to my expectations. Nothing in life would come to you without a higher education and no, that dancing shit that she was into wasn't good enough for me. From kindergarten through twelfth grade, Zalana did exceptionally well. Nothing less than a B minus graced her report cards and that was even better than the grades Banks earned.

I always thought my little girl would go on to become a lawyer, doctor, nurse, or engineer. Instead, she discarded her full ride merit scholarships and went on tour like a fucking jezebel. When Zalana injured her ankle my annoyance only grew further because that was exactly what I didn't want to happen. She threw away a foolproof plan for some shit that could be stripped from you at any moment. Shaking the thoughts about Zalana off, I opened the message and the sight before me made vomit rise in my throat.

KNOCK! KNOCK!

"Ezra, are you going to be in here all night? I'd like to cuddle with my husband tonight. Not my silk pillows." Zenobia questioned, entering my office. Fumbling around with my phone, I exited the video and stared up at her. I was positive that I resembled a deer caught in headlights because I couldn't let her view that video. She would call her father and that would just make this shit worse. The ransom video had one simple request that I was positive I could deliver and I was going to do just that. "What are you hiding on your phone?" She charged in my direction, fury in her eyes. "You in here talking to another bitch? Let me see so I can fuck you up!"

"Zenobia, I don't have time for your antics right now," I locked my phone and gripped her hands. Pushing her back into the wall, I kept a tight grip on Zenobia's wrists. She guzzled down quite a few glasses of wine with dinner and if I released her hands, she would definitely assault me. Zenobia's sudden increase in alcohol consumption was getting under my skin and I wasn't even sure how to address the situation.

"Well let me see Ezra! If you aren't working late then you're at the office! I don't feel loved anymore so who are you giving your love to? Why did you rush to put your phone up as soon as I entered the office? Let me fucking see!" She demanded, kicking her feet at me.

One of her knees collided with my stomach and it damn near knocked the wind out of me. Between the thoughts regarding the video and Zenobia's drinking swirling around in my head, I was about to lose my shit in here. Tossing Zenobia into my office chair, I stormed out of the house and rushed to Banks' house.

Banging on his front door, I waited for him to answer but it was taking too long. Using my spare key I barged into his home and regretted that shit. The sight of my son getting his dick sucked on the couch made me spin around.

"What the fuck pops?! That key is for emergencies only!" Banks complained to my back. "Go upstairs. I'll be up there in a minute," he directed at the young lady.

"Nah, she gotta go. This is an emergency," I explained.

"Alright shorty. You heard the man, slide out."

Shaking my head, I hated the way Banks treated these women but I didn't have time to lecture him about that right now. I'd told Banks at least a thousand times that he needed to find a nice girl and settle down instead of sticking his dick everywhere. He was going to either end up with an STD or a baby mama from hell if he kept it up. As stingy as Banks was, a mouth to feed was the last thing he needed.

A few minutes later the young lady brushed past me and exited the townhouse. I'm sure she was embarrassed as I was mortified for her ass. "Wassup pops?" Banks inquired after locking the door behind the young lady.

"I was reviewing my case files for tomorrow when I received this video from your sister's phone number," I detailed before showing him the video.

My baby girl sat on a leather sofa, dressed in the same dress she stormed out of the house wearing on New Year's Eve. Her hair was all over her head and dried tear stains were spread over her face. *"As you can see from her attire, we have had Zalana since New Year's Eve but we are keeping her safe. Our demands are simple, we heard you haven't been putting your best foot forward on Mario Lucero's case. Make sure you win his case in court tomorrow, your daughter's life depends on it."*

"What the fuck?!" Banks growled. "Did you call the police?"

"You think I should call the police? That might make shit worse," I faltered. "Throughout my years as a criminal defense attorney, I've witnessed a lot of shit. Plus being married to your mother, the offspring of a kingpin, I learned a great amount as well. These types of people are lawless and won't hesitate to kill your sister if they are backed into a corner."

"Well we should call grandpa. He can probably help us or tell us what the fuck to do," Banks advised me and I nodded my head in agreement. "Do you think you are going to win the case tomorrow?"

"I am very confident in the case. The state's evidence is weak and I've already poked plenty of holes in the case. It's usually against my policy to allow my clients to testify because even the slightest discrepancy or outburst of anger can kill your case. However, Mario insisted, he got on that stand and told his side of the story and promised there wouldn't be any issues or slip ups. I told him I didn't think it was a good idea so maybe that's what this is about."

"What type of man is your client?"

"From what I've gathered, he is the son of a mafia boss and you know they have connections out of this world. I need a drink," I wavered, my voice cracking. "I can't believe this is happening after how hard I was being on Zalana a few days ago."

"It's going to be okay, pops," Banks assured me, rushing into the kitchen. "Where is mom?"

"I didn't tell her, I couldn't. You know how she can be and I didn't want her panicking and making the situation worse. That's why I came over here."

"Yeah, you right, mom shouldn't know right now. I'm going to call grandpa and some of the people I know that may be able to help us without official police interference. I'll ask grandpa not to tell mom but when grandpa gets here, he might decide to tell her anyways and nothing can stop that. The good thing is he will be here to keep her in check since that seems to be the only person that she listens to."

"Banks, I'm never going to be able to forgive myself for this shit. Your mother won't and I'm sure Zalana won't either. Your mother already says I am sacrificing our relationship for my career and all types of shit. I love you, your sister, and your mother more than anything," I sobbed, placing my head into the palms of my hands. The chickens were coming home to roost and I prayed that Zalana would make her way out of this situation. I threw back the generous amount of D'Usse that Banks handed me and stood up to pace the floor while he made the calls.

Time kept ticking, my nerves were getting worse by the hour and I still had to go into this courtroom and put on my best defense. Banks was about my size and I was able to throw on one of his suits with the Stacy Adams I wore to his house last night. After a long sleepless evening and a cup of coffee we were on our way out of the door for the morning. I headed to the courthouse and Banks went to pick his grandfather up from the airport.

Entering the courthouse, I immediately spotted Mario's father and approached him. He was an average sized man but his deadly eyes made him appear scary. "Good morning, Mr. Lucero. I just want you to know that I got your message and I'm going to win this case."

He nodded his head and patted me on the back. "I sure hope so."

"If your son insists on testifying then I can call him to the stand but he has to do his part and keep his cool. His testimony could break a case that we are already winning. In my expert opinion, I think that it is best for everyone involved if he avoids the witness stand."

"At this point, it's your call," he shrugged and walked off.

I knew I was making the right decision for his son and my daughter, they would see in the end.

BANKS

My grandfather's tall frame sauntered through the automatic doors with agitation displayed on every inch of his face. Zachariah Freeman was the man to see in the streets of Tampa back in the day but left the streets alone and relocated to Reno, Nevada when he retired. Even at his age, anyone that caught a glimpse of him would immediately realize that he wasn't one to fuck with. Grandpa had some strong ass genes too because I inherited my height, weight, and looks from my grandfather. As grandpa approached my truck, the harsh reality washed over me.

I couldn't tell you how many times I'd picked my grandpa up from the airport. On the previous occasions, I met him with a bottle of his favorite, E&J, and a blunt rolled. This time I was empty handed and couldn't form a smile for shit. Zalana was my baby, she was my responsibility, and I should've gone after her. Instead I stayed home and continued drinking with my niggas while my sister was out there suffering. I guess my mother's intuitions were correct and that was going to make shit worse when she found out the truth. She told us that something was wrong and we told her that she was tripping. Now we were in a fucked up position, starting damn near three days behind whoever kidnapped my sister. I wasn't a killer, thug, or none of that shit, but I was willing to do a lot of things behind my sister.

Exiting my whip, I walked around and embraced my grandfather in a hug. He tossed his duffle bag into my backseat and we returned to our respective sides of the truck. "Tell me everything you know?" Grandpa requested, easing into my Denali.

I regurgitated every detail that I had as we drove back to my place. My grandfather was older but he was still respected in these streets. I experienced it first hand because it was off the strength of his name that I was able to secure my connect for the cocaine I used to funnel through my club. There was no time like now to have an OG of the streets on your side. Once grandpa was brought up to speed, he made a few calls and directed me through traffic until we arrived at an open field.

"I'm only allowing you to tag along because this is a dire situation. Don't go looking for any of these niggas to buy drugs from behind my back. Ya hear me?" Grandpa questioned as I threw the truck in park.

"Never doing that shit again. I just want to find my sister," I replied.

"I ain't leaving the city until my princess is home," he confirmed, exiting the truck.

I followed grandpa's lead and approached the men. "A few of you have already met my grandson Banks, don't let that shit happen again," his eyes swiveled in Perry's direction. When I was funneling drugs through my nightclub I was buying them from Perry. He nodded his head in confirmation and my grandpa continued. "When I left the streets alone, I thought that was the safest thing I could do for my family. Clearly that wasn't the case because somebody snatched my granddaughter, Zalana. Do any of y'all know anything about that shit?"

The four men all denied any involvement and my grandpa continued. "Who is working with the Luceros? I need to know where I can find their people, trap houses, stash houses, anything."

"Shit, we ain't heard about them moving weight out here and none of us are working with them and we got this portion of the state on lock," Vinny expressed. "I heard about one of their boys on trial for murder but from my understanding, he was visiting his baby mama when he got arrested out here. They got motion down south, Miami, Fort Lauderdale and shit, but not up here."

"Y'all sure about that?" Grandpa eyed them.

"Absolutely. We wouldn't lie to you. If them motha fuckas got your granddaughter just say the word and we got y'all back," Marcello affirmed.

"Bet." Grandpa acknowledged before turning towards the truck.

Trailing behind him silently, I didn't know what we were doing next but I was down for whatever. My phone rang and it was my father calling. "Hello."

"Hey Banks, did your grandfather make it here yet?"

"Yeah, he's in the passenger seat right now."

"Good. The jury is going out to deliberate and I'm headed home. I have at least a hundred missed calls from your mom. I'm going to tell her what's going on since your grandpa is here to check her ass. Can y'all meet me at the house?"

"Yeah, we are going to head over there now."

"See you there."

We ended the call and I changed course as my grandfather clicked around on a flip phone. If I could trust anyone, it was grandpa and I knew how he was coming behind Zalana so this shit was just getting started.

CHAPTER ELEVEN

Streetz

Zalana sat on the couch nervous as shit and I couldn't blame her. It took the jury two days to finally return with a *not guilty* verdict and that was nearly six hours ago. Since then this nigga Redd hadn't been able to contact the motha fuckas who hired him for the job. I was scheduled to meet the landlord of the new crib I was moving to in an hour so he had thirty minutes to get in touch and collect the other half of his bread before I let this girl go. This was not how I planned to start my New Year at the fuck all.

The rest of the niggas that were helping Redd on what looked to be a dummy mission were on the porch smoking weed. After another unanswered call, Redd joined them niggas on the porch while I rolled up another blunt for myself.

"Tall Man, are y'all really going to let me go after I saw your face?" Zalana peered at me with squinted eyes.

Her body was tense and I swear I needed to get the fuck away from this girl. She was breathtakingly beautiful with a pair of perfect lips and innocent eyes positioned perfectly on her caramel face. It wasn't just her beauty though, when I held the blunt up to Zalana's lips, I promise I felt a connection the way she stared back at me. After spending the last forty-eight hours with her on this couch, I'd witnessed her goofy smile a few times and I needed to stop craving that shit. Especially when I knew I'd never experience this shit again and the feelings I had were conjured up in my dysfunctional ass mind.

All Zalana wanted to do was get the fuck away from me. Then I thought back to the nickname she'd called me, Tall Man, I never let anybody call me anything other than Streetz. However, I loved when she referred to me as Tall Man so I let that shit rock. Maybe she didn't view me as a dangerous monster, I guess only time would tell. For some reason, I knew my head viewed her as something we'd been missing while my dick thought she was something we had to have. Shaking those thoughts out of my head, I took a deep breath and answered the question that she was mulling over.

"We are going to let you go. I already told that nigga he got another thirty minutes and that's it. Relax, I don't make promises that I can't keep. I've done enough shit in life to earn a seat under the jail. If you decide to snitch on me after how nicely I've treated you then it is what it is," I shrugged.

"Is that the only reason you've been so nice to me?" She pondered.

"What?"

"Have you only been nice to me because I saw your face?"

"Nah, I just ain't the type of nigga to sit back and allow a man to harm a woman," I explained.

"So you really aren't worried about me telling on you?"

"Nah, I just did a year and a day in prison, that shit don't scare me. Plus I don't have shit to live for so it won't be a problem to sit down for a minute. It's that or kill you and I ain't letting that go down," I shrugged and looked into her eyes. "You got my word."

"Although your words were grim, I still don't like the *hopelessness* filling your tone. Don't say things like that because..."

"Aye, don't worry about what the fuck I let fly outta my mouth. You don't know me like that," I snapped on her. As soon as the words left my mouth, I regretted it. Zalana immediately cowered on the couch and I hated that she suddenly feared me. The entire time we'd been thrust into this situation, Zalana never looked at me with fear like she did just now. Her eyes were usually anxious or wondering but never fearful. Realizing that I fucked up, I stood from the couch and decided to end this shit. I need to let Zalana go, my black ass was probably holding onto her until the deadline because I developed some sort of crush.

"I appreciate you for looking out for me," Zalana expressed.

"Yeah," I reverted to my short answers before exiting the house. "Yo, call that motha fucka one more time and if they don't answer, take that L and move the fuck on. You shouldn't have been into this type of shit anyways."

"What? You done made your girlfriend mad, now you wanna get rid of her?" Redd joked.

"Alright, fuck it. I'mma just let her go then," I shrugged and opened the front door.

"Come on. I'm about to drop you off wherever you wanna go," I commanded.

Zalana jolted from the couch and darted towards the front door with her slippers clacking along the way. "Aye, this is the second time that car spun the block," Breon explained.

I turned around to assess the situation and gunshots rang out before I could view the car. Zalana stood frozen in place, forcing me to tackle her ass when I should've been bussin' back. Covering Zalana's body with mine, I reached for my gun as she screamed at the top of her fuckin' lungs. Her screams were laced with terror and that shit pissed me off. I was ready to buss back but I heard tires squealing before I could end them niggas. If Zalana wasn't here them niggas would've been as good as dead.

Peeling myself off of Zalana, I hovered over her, patting around on her body. I was examining her for gunshot wounds because her deafening screams persisted. "Where the girl at?" I heard someone shout on the porch before additional gunshots erupted. An unfamiliar man entered the home and I pulled the trigger, sending a bullet straight through his head. His body plopped down to the middle of the floor and I kneeled down next to Zalana.

"Come here, it's over," I pulled her from the floor and into my arms. The hug was short lived because I had to get the fuck on and I couldn't let Zalana go now. Gripping Zalana's hand, I drug her outside and quickly processed that Redd, Santiago, and Breon were all deceased. Running through all three of their pockets, I confiscated the burner phones that would incriminate me. Scooping Zalana off of her feet, I jogged over to my Impala and slid her into the passenger seat. Speeding away from the house, I checked my rearview mirror consistently to ensure that we weren't being followed.

"Outside of being a lawyer, what other shit is your pops into?" I grilled her, maneuvering through the one lane roads at top speed. Zalana sat in the seat crying and fidgeting in her seat. "Aye, snap out of that shit. What other shit is your pops into? Why would he send some niggas to find you instead of calling the police?"

"I don't know!" Zalana shouted at me then I saw a realization slap her ass in the middle of her lil tantrum.

"Spit that shit out!" I barked, hopping onto the interstate. "Prior to them niggas spraying the spot, my only concern was prison if you went back and ran yo mouth but now I gotta worry about a nigga gunnin' for my top. If you can't tell me shit, Ion know if I'll be able to keep my word, at least not until I figure out who your people really are. I need to know what I'm up against before I let you go."

"It was my grandfather," she murmured.

"Grandfather?" I puzzled, glancing at her for a moment.

"Yeah, he used to be in the streets before he retired. My daddy is just a lawyer but I'm sure they called my grandfather after they received that ransom video."

"What's his name?"

"Zachariah Freeman," she confessed.

"Big Z is your grandfather?"

She nodded in agreement while I shook my head. The name was one I'd heard on more than a few occasions. Although Zachariah was before my time and I never met or conducted business with him, I was well versed in the motha fuckas that preceded me. I didn't know who would go against the grain and hire some dumb motha fuckas to kidnap his granddaughter but it wasn't a conundrum I had time to dissect.

"Please let me go home, I promise I won't tell anyone about you. I can just say that I got loose after the shootout. Pleaseeeee Tall Man, you have my word."

"You don't have to do all of that. Ion wanna leave you on the side of the road and I ain't pulling up to your crib either," I mulled over my next choice until she interrupted me.

"Ummmm, take me to a fire station," Zalana suggested.

"A fire station?"

"Yeah, when parents want to safely give their babies up, they are supposed to take them to the fire station. Someone is always there and there are no questions asked. Just take me there, no questions asked and I can go inside and have someone take me home."

Taking a deep breath, I didn't know what else to do and I needed to get the fuck out of town after what just went down. Passing Zalana my phone, I guess we would go along with her plan. "Find the nearest fire station I can take you to."

Zalana snatched the phone and clicked around until she located our destination. I maneuvered through traffic, following the directions from my phone until we arrived at the fire station. To be on the safe side I spun the block, ensuring there wasn't anyone outside of the fire station to see her get out of my car. Easing up to the curb down the block, I verified a clear line of sight to the front door of the fire station before turning to Zalana.

"Be safe, protect yourself, and I apologize for inadvertently playing a part in this situation." I nodded my head.

"Thank you!" Zalana celebrated and hugged me. Her soft skin brushed up against mine and the desire to make her stay increased the longer Zalana held onto me. This was the most affection I welcomed in a long time as I wrapped my arms around Zalana to hug her back for as long as she would let me. Luckily I wasn't a delusional ass nigga or else I might've told her ass she couldn't leave, this position was just that comforting. Zalana pulled away from me and offered a soft smile to which I countered with a headnod before exiting the car.

She sprinted across the street as if I was going to change my mind. I enjoyed the sight of her fat ass bouncing with each movement across the grass that led to the front door of the fire station. When Zalana opened the door, she paused for a moment and glanced over her shoulder, our eyes connected for a brief moment before she stepped inside. I sped away from the curb and headed back to the interstate. There really wasn't shit here for me so I might as well make a quick move until shit cooled down and I knew for sure if Zalana would keep her word about concealing my identity.

CHAPTER TWELVE

Zalana

3 Months Later
April 2022

*R*ight, left, left, right, knee. I chanted to myself while assaulting the torso training bag as my father, Banks, and the trainer they'd hired observed from a distance. My daily routine now incorporated some form of self-defense after being kidnapped and my weekly routine included a forty-five minute therapy session. I frequented the gym and gun range so much that I wished I never had to see them again. Healing myself was a complex journey because my parents insisted that I move back in with them until further notice and I felt like I was a prisoner all over again. They were concerned, I get it, but I was running away from their asses before I was kidnapped.

"Your skills have improved tremendously from our initial training session," Edward, the self defense trainer, complimented me.

Sweat dripped off every inch of my body and I fought to catch my breath. I was putting in work and it was torture on my body, secretly I would've rather been at the gun range. Pulling the trigger was so much easier than this shit but my brother and father always said I needed to be able to protect myself in spaces where I couldn't bring my gun. My natural curls wiggled their way out of my loose bun and hung wildly, making my neck and shoulders hotter. With my breathing under control, I pulled my hair back up into a bun. Edward passed me a bottle of water and I accepted, drinking a generous amount before plopping in the middle of the grass.

"That's all for today. I'll see you on Friday," Edward explained, gathering his equipment from the grass.

"You will not, I am taking my life back and going on a girls' trip."

"You what?" My father gasped. "Aye, I'mma call you right back," he ended the call he stepped to the side to answer and addressed me.

"You not going on no fucking girls' trip! Have you lost your mind?" Banks added in.

"I'm going on this trip. Since the moment I got back, y'all have been smothering me!" I exclaimed, thinking back to the day Tall Man let me out at the fire station.

After barging through the doors of the fire station, I told them my story and they sprung into action. An hour later I was seated in a hospital bed, against my will because I told them I wasn't harmed, but they insisted. My family trickled in, a few police officers were investigating, and the FBI also got involved.

Armed with my detailed statement, the case was ongoing with little real answers due to the three kidnappers being found deceased at the home they held me captive in. As promised, I left Tall Man out of my story and the only question now was who shot up the house during my last day in captivity. According to my grandfather, he didn't send men to the house that day. In fact, grandpa was on his way to meet with the head of the Lucero Mob to verify their involvement and demand my safe return. Plus grandpa assured me that he wouldn't have allowed anyone to shoot at a house that his princess was being held in. The worst part about it all was my name and face being plastered all over the news, also against my wishes. I didn't want the entire world all up in my business but it was too late for that shit.

Although I didn't venture out of my parents' house often, when I did, the sympathetic stares from people that recognized my face from the news were suffocating. My family assumed I didn't leave the house because I was fearful of being abducted again when in reality, it was the stares that kept me inside. The FBI was researching connections between Mario Lucero and the men who kidnapped me but there wasn't anything solid the last time they checked in with us. Grandpa had a sit down with the head of the Lucero Mob who assured them that they weren't involved in my kidnapping. Whoever hired the men to kidnap me was smart, they paid in cash and communicated on a throw away phone. Grandpa went home for a little while to check on his property and this was my time to run for it because he was the only elder in the family that could convince me to sit my ass down.

It was my lucky day because Yola and the ladies from her shop were going to Atlanta for the Bronner Brothers Hair Show. Over the last three months, Yola checked on me consistently, she felt terrible when the news broke about my kidnapping after leaving the club. When she mentioned that she was going to Atlanta this weekend I didn't hesitate to invite myself on the trip. Yola welcomed me with open arms and I was tagging along. I needed a break from my family, they were smothering me, real bad.

Edward scurried out of the backyard, giving us privacy, and my mother sauntered out of the backdoor with her usual glass of wine in her hand. When you saw me, you saw my phone clasped tightly in the palms of my hand; when you encountered my mama, she had a glass of wine in her hand. I wasn't one to judge, but the shit did seem a little excessive now that I was residing in the home with my parents.

"What are y'all fussing about?"

Her question was directed at all three of us, but I wasn't listening to shit my brother and father had to say. "I'm going out of town with Yola and the other ladies that work in her shop. I'm not going to remain confined to the property lines at this address for the rest of my life. It's been three months, I took the class to obtain my concealed carry permit. I bought a gun to keep at home and one that remains in my purse. I'm even out here sweating my behind off training with Edward four times a week. The next step is freedom and I'm about to have a little slice of it this weekend."

"Are you sure, Zalana?" My mom questioned, her jovial expression flipped to one of apprehension.

"I don't want you guys to worry about me while I'm gone but I need to get back into the swing of life," I lamented, approaching my mother. "We can't live the rest of our life in fear. I am grown, I will protect myself and be sure of my surroundings. Plus I will be with my girls the entire time I'm gone, leaving no room for error."

"Zalana, you just met this Yola girl. How can we know you can trust her? I've been on her social media page since you guys have been getting closer and I don't like some of her antics. She's very wild, what is this trip going to be like?"

"Ma, I am a good judge of character and can decide who will be my friends. Plus this is also a trip that I will learn from, Yola owns a successful beauty lounge and we are going to a hair show. I love you but I need to shower so I can meet up with the ladies at Yola's shop. We are driving up to Atlanta in a Sprinter van so I can bring my gun and other things without an issue. It's going to be fine. I'll have maybe one or two drinks and that's it."

"No drinks at all," my mom retorted. I fought the urge to roll my eyes and tell her she had some nerve. Instead, I offered a head nod and a hug before rushing past her into the house. Banks started lecturing my mother as I entered the house but I didn't care, it was time to get back into the swing of life and Atlanta was the perfect place to do that. I would be free of the sympathetic stares because people wouldn't recognize me out of town.

After packing my bags, Banks begrudgingly transported me to Yola's shop and gave all of us a lecture like he was our fucking daddy. I was so happy when Yola's husband stepped in and said one of his people was driving the Sprinter van and would watch out for us during our trip. That also gave me an added sense of security and I was ready to hit these Atlanta streets and enjoy myself.

10 O'CLOCK SATURDAY NIGHT

Watching Yola and her girls do their thing at the Bronner Brothers Hair Show made me admire their craft even more. It also made me think about my own dreams more. Being surrounded by all of those beautiful black thriving entrepreneurs was exhilarating. While I was cooped up in my childhood bedroom I spent my free time preparing a business plan, budget, and savings goals to work towards opening my dance studio. When I got back I was going to ask my grandpa for the money against my parents' wishes and if that didn't work, I would go the loan route next.

"It's time to slide ladiessssss!" Yola yelled, walking through the Airbnb with shot glass necklaces and a bottle of Casamigos. "But before we make our departure, you must take shots! I love and appreciate you guys for coming along and representing Yo's Beauty Lounge today and everyday," she detailed, passing out her shot glass necklaces and Casamigos. Me and Yola's sister Anya were the last ones in the room to receive a necklace but she didn't pour any liquor into our tiny cups like she did the other women. "Y'all are on a reduced liquor schedule. I'm glad y'all are next to each other. Zalana, your brother was on one yesterday and my husband promised that we would watch over you and bring you home in one piece." Yola explained before turning to her sister. "Anya, your husband made me swear that you wouldn't get too drunk because he needs you in tip top shape to help with y'all bad ass child when he gets home..."

"Don't call my baby bad," Anya chuckled, snatching the bottle from Yola. She drank a swig straight from the bottle. "And this is my kid free time, I'm drinking all the liquor."

"Turn up on them hoes then bae!" Yola screeched and Anya started twerking.

Not one to kill the vibes, I took the bottle from Yola and swallowed a small amount before leading the group to the bus. We went to Magic City, where we consumed more liquor and food while supporting the naked hustle. It was my first time in a strip club so I was in awe, soaking it all up. Beautiful naked women, ones flying everywhere and it was a vibe. I did have a few drinks but avoided the blunts that were in rotation because I wanted to keep my promise to not get fucked up while we were in Atlanta.

We left the club thirty minutes before they closed and I was happy because my feet were screaming in my stilettos. Clearly wearing sneakers over the last three months allowed me to forget the struggles that came with heels. Beauty took pain though because I was wearing the fuck out of these new stilettos. I might have been confined to the gym or my parents' home but I was definitely running up a tab on my mom's credit cards.

The driver was waiting for us at the door before we made our exit and escorted us to the awaiting ride. When Dro said his boy was going to watch over us, he did just that. Stepping onto the bus, the party was still going as Yola turned the music up and *Big Booty* by Gucci Mane blared through the speakers. Standing on the seats, I danced with the other ladies and let loose, drinking more shots because I felt safe on our way back to the Airbnb. I wanted to be as turnt as the rest of the gang. When we were a few minutes away from the spot, Yola asked the driver to stop at a QuickTrip for snacks.

Scavenging the aisles, I grabbed a Sprite, sour cream and onion Lays, two Snickers, and a blunt before checking out. Although I didn't smoke weed in the club, I definitely needed a blunt before bed. I was now a two blunt a day type of bitch since the kidnapping and I needed that shit to help me fall asleep and start my day. When we exited the store the music from the Sprinter van spilled into the parking lot. This ratchet weekend was exactly what I needed.

CHAPTER THIRTEEN

Streetz

"*F*uck, fuck, fuck." I sighed after combing through the top drawer of the night stand, searching for a blunt.

There was supposed to be one pack of Grabba Leafs left for me to roll up before taking my ass to sleep but clearly I must've miscalculated. Sleep never came easy to me and tonight was no different, I needed that blunt to help me catch some z's. Slipping out of the bed, I grabbed my phone and keys then exited the lil apartment I was staying in. Since releasing Zalana, I took a trip out of town, far enough to be away from the city, but close enough to collect my paper on a weekly basis. During my incarceration Redd collected my cash but now that he was gone, there wasn't a soul alive that I would trust with my shit. I had to make the trip back home tomorrow to collect my bread and wanted to be well rested to do so.

Redd's mother, my Aunt Victoria, kept calling my phone, asking for answers about what happened to her son. I knew Victoria had a TV and watched the news. Her son's face was in rotation for a few weeks while they reported on Zalana's kidnapping story, the nigga was a deceased kidnapper, nothing more and nothing less. That shit also had me on edge and I had to change up my number on her ass. We hadn't held a conversation since I was a jit and I didn't plan on rekindling shit with her ass now. I understood that Redd was her son but she despised my ass all of these years. I didn't give a fuck that her son was deceased, she had to keep that same energy and stand on those feelings she had when I was a jit. Hell, Redd didn't even know I was his big cousin until they were strapped for cash. Knowing who I was in the streets, Aunt Vickie knew she couldn't ask me for shit but sending my twenty year old cousin my way for a spot on the team was her only option. Although I knew that was the plan, I still gave his dumb ass a chance because he was my lil cousin and shouldn't be held accountable for his mother's deplorable actions. After the way everything played out, I should've continued to treat that nigga like a stranger.

Even if I wanted to speak to her ass, I couldn't provide her answers in regards to Redd's murder anyways. That nigga was involved in some shit that he should've never been apart of and that led to his demise. I never asked who hired him because I didn't give a fuck. Kidnapping bitches for a fee like he was hurting for cash, that green hoe greed was a motha fucka and cost Redd his life. Shit, that motha fucka could've got me killed or sent up the road, I was gone have to deal with that nigga regardless once the entire situation was over. In my line of work I couldn't afford to have sneaky, reckless niggas operating in my back-yard. I gave Redd a chance to make some money to take care of his wicked ass mama and he got in above his head, that was on him.

Pushing that bullshit to the back of my mind, I took a short ride to the QuickTrip. Slow rolling into the parking lot, I thought my eyes were playing tricks on me when I spotted Zalana's ass in a crowd full of hoes dancing in front of a Sprinter van while one of them recorded. Circling the parking lot, I chose to park at the gas pump on the oppo-site side of the ladies. Killing my engine, I stepped out of the car and Zalana sashayed in front of the chick that was recording.

"We all in Atlanta with it! Tampa shit hoessss!" She referred to the song *Going Crazy* by Tae Bae Bae that was booming through the speakers.

Zalana was clearly drunk or tipsy, sticking her middle finger up in front of the camera. I watched from afar for a moment, intrigued, turned on, and lowkey pissed were all emotions that I was experi-encing simultaneously. Zalana was wearing a tight ass dress that clung to her body and baby girl was stacked. Her hair was different, big natural curls flowed about her head, and I liked that shit a hundred times better than that straight hair she wore when I first met her.

That smile Zalana wore was contagious. I caught a half smile here and there at the trap house but right now she was cheesing so motha fuckin' hard, showing all her teeth and gums for the camera. This girl was gorgeous and above all else true to her word. I wouldn't have been mad if Zalana went back and told her grandpa or the police about me. However, she didn't and that made Zalana solid. Zalana took over for the camera girl, grabbing the phone with her back to me and her guards clearly down. Shaking my head, I swaggered across the parking lot and pulled her into my chest from behind.

"After everything you've been through, you really out here inebriated with your guards down. No gun or nothing, just a fuckin' phone," I whispered in her ear as she squirmed her way out of my grasp.

Zalana was floating, I could tell by the way she looked up at me with her eyes all squinted tight. "Tall Man?"

"Boy, unhand my friend! What the fuck is you a perv or something?" I heard a female yell.

"Shut the fuck up!" I barked back as a reflex. My eyes remained trained on Zalana so I didn't know who was talking shit and I really didn't give a fuck.

"Nigga, who the fuck you talking too?!" She barreled towards us with some nigga on her heels.

"It's cool, Yola," Zalana assured her.

I finally glanced her way and immediately recognized who it was. "My bad Yola, I didn't recognize you and definitely didn't expect to see you all the way from home. Does your husband know you out here acting a fool?"

"Mind the business that pays you Streetz, you cool with my husband not me," Yola stuck her middle finger up at me and grabbed the nigga that was with them. She better have, if he would've come too close, he was gone end up bleeding out in this parking lot. "Zalana, are you staying with him or going with us?"

Zalana looked over her shoulder at me and I offered her a gentle headnod. "I'm going with him."

"Make sure you get her back to us by three o'clock tomorrow because that's when we are hitting the road. Don't make no babies!" Yola waved at us before climbing onto the Sprinter van.

"You got a blunt in yo bag?" I inquired.

"Yep," she nodded her head, offering a shy smile.

Gripping Zalana's hand, I led her over to my whip and opened the passenger door to ensure that her drunk ass got in safely. I never thought I would see her again, I dreamt about this shit on a few different occasions and none of those dreams could've compared to the actual moment. My heart beat differently when I was around this woman and that was some shit I didn't understand. If I'm being honest, I didn't care to understand, I just wanted to feel that shit. Pulling into my assigned parking spot, I turned the lights on in the car and cupped Zalana's chin.

"You don't have to come in here if you don't want to. I can take you back to your people," I offered.

"No... Ummm... I want to be here," she faltered, her eyes darting everywhere except for in my face.

I released her chin and took a deep breath. "Then why you don't sound sure about it?"

"It's weird." Zalana unbuckled her seat belt and leaned back in the seat. I waited intently as she stared at the roof of the car. "I've been to therapy and everything because outside of a stranger who can't tell nobody shit I say, I've been burying how I feel inside and hiding the fact that I think about you a lot. You made me feel safe and although this sounds crazy, I enjoyed being around you and talking with you over the few blunts we shared. Ughhhhhh, the bar is so fuckin' low, it's in hell but I don't care right now." Zalana rambled then tried to maneuver herself to my side of the car but I gripped her arms and pushed her back to her seat.

"Chill out."

Opening my door, I slid out of the car and walked around to help Zalana out. Leading her into my space, I wasn't sure what would come next for us, but I was prepared for anything. Trailing behind Zalana, I caught a whiff of her and she smelled delectable, making my dick hard. Sitting my keys and phone on the table, I tried to reposition myself but her ass wasn't drunk enough to miss it when she brushed past me to claim a seat on the couch. "Is that a glock in your pants or is he happy to see me?"

Shaking my head, I pulled the bag from her grasp and dug around for something to roll this weed up with. She had a pack of Swishers, I hated rolling with them, but it would do for the night. Zalana received a call from her friends, probably checking in to make sure that she was straight while I sparked up the blunt. When she ended the call, we smoked the blunt together, awkward silence filling the air until we were finished. Zalana asked to take a shower and I led her to the bathroom where everything she needed was laid out and passed her a t-shirt to put on.

Laying back in bed, I rolled another blunt while waiting for Zalana to handle her business. When she re-entered the room, her bubbly ass bounced on the bed and landed in my lap. Her ass hung out the bottom of her shorts while her titties bounced all over. She knew what the fuck she was doing. Taking a deep breath, the gentleman in me went out of the window. Wrapping my arms around her back, I flipped her over and pinned her down on the bed. As bad as I wanted to rearrange her insides, I kept my dick in my pants. She leaned up and kissed me and I swear that shit made me feel alive, an intense yearning for Zalana shot through me. My lips trailed down Zalana's neck and the sexy ass panting she was doing turned a nigga on even more. Caressing her titties with both of my hands, I continued trailing my tongue further south until I was face to face with her pussy.

This fat motha fucka was perfect and I felt her clit jump when I flicked my tongue across it. Trailing my tongue from Zalana's clit to her pussy slit, I dug my tongue inside. Using my thumb to massage her clit, I tongue fucked her pussy, enjoying the sweet nectar her body secreted.

"Shit! Right there," she moaned, ecstasy dripping off of each syllable.

Zalana's hands rummaged through my plats, massaging my scalp until she grabbed a handful of my hair and I had to pull my head back and use my free hand to remove her grasp. I was willing to do a lot of shit to keep Zalana in my life and make up for the way we met, but I wasn't no bitch so hair pulling was out of the equation. Swiftly switching my tongue and thumb's positions once she got the hint, I sucked on her clit and allowed my middle and index finger to explore her insides. Zalana's persistent moans were as beautiful as the rhythm to which she grinded her pussy into my face. "I'm about to cum!" Zalana shouted and I made sure to spell my name across her clit before her body went limp in my mouth.

Peering up at Zalana, she offered me a drowsy smile. Grinning back up at her, I slid up behind her. "Take yo beautiful ass to sleep." I pecked her cheek and pulled her back into my chest.

"I swear that sounded so good rolling off the tip of your tongue," Zalana cooed, turning over to plant a kiss on my lips. Caressing Zalana's ass, I spun her around because I was a millisecond away from shedding this gentleman facade and fucking the shit out of her.

"For real, beautiful, let's go to sleep. Your friends gave me a return time and I'm trying to meet it."

"Good night," she sighed. "I hope I don't wake up and this shit is all a drunken dream. My pussy can't take another wet dream."

Chuckling, I snuggled my head into the crook of Zalana's neck and silently waited for her to fall asleep. Now that I had Zalana in my bed, sleep definitely wasn't going to come to me this evening because my dreams were now a reality and I knew the shit would be over soon. How the fuck could we be after our initial meeting? That was some shit we would have to take to the grave and I couldn't see that happening with us running around like a pair of smitten puppies.

CHAPTER FOURTEEN
Shadae

Since I discovered meditation after my abortion, the therapeutic measure became a part of my daily routine. December 2021 was a dark time for me, I allowed my parents to convince me that the baby I was carrying wouldn't thrive with me and Streetz as unwed parents. Then I lost Streetz, my best friend and the love of my life, to the prison system the day after terminating my pregnancy. After it was all said and done I went back to the home I shared with Streetz daily and mourned my pregnancy alone. To make matters worse, an enormous box from Amazon filled with keepsake items for the baby arrived a day after Streetz was arrested.

I fucked up and I knew it. I stripped myself, my baby, and Streetz of a future that we would never be able to explore the possibilities. My parents didn't give a fuck about the emotional turmoil I was in, they expected me to move on because they didn't feel like Streetz was good enough to be a father. Looking back, I should've listened to Streetz and kept my ass home for Christmas. That day led to the downward spiral that I found myself on.

During the first few months of Streetz's incarceration I used liquor to cope with my feelings after the abortion. Liquor and loneliness led to a short but quiet fling with a bartender from my favorite bar and a few other men I now regretted involving myself with. When I finally got myself out of that situation I met Banks. He was so fine, caring, and we had similar personality types so it was easy for me to fall for Banks while waiting for Streetz to come home. Although Streetz was my best friend before we decided to cross that line, we differed in personality. Streetz was a homebody and enjoyed being home, alone in solitude while I loved exploring new places and exposing myself to different experiences.

Banks was so sweet prior to Streetz's release from prison. We went on dates, explored the city and surrounding area together, watched movies after I got off of work, and I even met his family on New Year's Eve. However, he changed up after we had sex. Initially, I assumed his shift in energy was due to the situation with Zalana being kidnapped.

After a few weeks of Banks avoiding me I ran into him while grabbing to go food from Green Lemon. He was sitting in a booth all hugged up and happy with some bitch. When I confronted Banks he made it clear we were just fucking and not building anything serious so his actions weren't any of my concern. That shit crushed my little feelings so I tossed both of the drinks from their table in his face and left without grabbing the food I already paid for. I was the one who introduced his disrespectful ass to Green Lemon and he had the nerve to be taking other bitches there. After leaving the restaurant Banks sent me a simple text message saying, **fuck you hoe, lose my number.** I went to reply to his text message and tell him that I was pregnant so he couldn't get rid of me that easily but he blocked me before I hit the send button.

Since then, I haven't heard from Banks and was fine with that. I had a lot of shit going on and the last thing I needed was stress from these niggas. My phone rang and I glanced at the screen, it was my mom calling but I didn't need the stress from my parents either. Dressed in my leggings and sports bra, I tugged my hot pink yoga mat off of the top shelf in my closet and lugged it out of my backdoor. I laid my yoga mat out on the grass and plopped down in a relaxing position. My backyard had a large Live Oak tree positioned off to the right, creating a nice breeze to combat the blazing April sun because it was in full swing.

Since learning of my pregnancy, the only time I seemed to have a little relief from the morning sickness was when I was outside. I opened the Apple Music app and opened the Yoga and Chill playlist to fill the backyard. Placing my phone at the bottom of the mat, I got in a comfortable seated position and took a couple deep breaths. My eyes popped open at the sound of my side gate opening and I was met with the intense gazes of my parents.

"We have been calling you all week," my mom expressed, stepping further into the backyard. When she got close enough to observe my body I saw the revelation send a wave of angst through her body. "You're pregnant?"

I almost wanted to lie to them because you had to really know me to see the changes in my body. The tell tale sign of my pregnancy was the slight pudge I'd grown when I used to have a super flat stomach. "But how? I thought that you and Samuel broke up right after he was released from prison. He had you wait for him to get out of prison just to get you pregnant and leave you once he was set free."

"It's not Streetz's baby," I blurted out, climbing to my feet.

"Well we need to understand what is going on. Why are you having unprotected sex with randoms?" My dad asked, raising my level of nausea and frustration. I didn't plan to tell my parents until I was super pregnant because I didn't want to hear their mouths or deal with their bullshit. Nothing was going as I felt it should have in my life so I burst into an emotional fit of tears.

"Why are you crying? You were doing grown acts so now is not the time to cry," my father badgered.

"I'm crying because of the hormones and you two are triggering me. I am already dealing with the reality that I'm single and pregnant and now you two are going to be on my back. To be honest, I just want you to leave me alone."

"Well that isn't going to happen," my father scoffed. "Go grab your shoes. We are going to pay the young man that you're pregnant by a visit and discuss this like adults. You guys are going to be a family now."

"No, I will take care of my child alone. This isn't the fifties, rolling up on him isn't going to force his hand."

"It takes two to tango, Shadae." I rolled my eyes at him using that old ass line. "We won't push abortion on you after what happened last time but the father will step up to the plate. Let's go!" His voice elevated with his request, causing me to jump. I didn't want to disobey my father but I also didn't want to take them to put anyone else in my business because I had too much going on right now. "Let's go, Shadae!"

Against my wishes, I stomped into the house to grab my shoes while trying to conjure up a way out of this situation without my parents knowing my business. Unfortunately, that was impossible with them hovering over me. My father was doing the talking while my mother stood by, quiet as a church mouse. We piled into my father's car and I directed them to Banks' house. As we neared Banks' home, I noticed my mother perk up at the sight of the area.

"He lives over here on Davis Island? What does he do for a living?"

"He owns a dispensary."

"That isn't ideal but it's clear that the business has been good to him. What type of family does he come from? Please tell me at least working class."

"His dad is a lawyer and his mom is a homemaker," I rolled my eyes. All they cared about was their careers, making sure that my life choices didn't embarrass them and maintaining some type of superiority to others.

It was Friday and Banks was usually at his dispensary and I prayed he kept his schedule and wasn't home. That way my father would feel like I attempted to do the right thing and move on to whatever else he had planned for this Sunday morning.

When we approached the address my heart dropped because not only was Banks home but he was outside smoking a blunt while walking another bitch to her car. She was beautiful too, skin the color of cocoa, natural kinky curls flowing in the wind. It was clear that Banks had a thing for the natural dark skinned women because I swear this hoe looked just like me and the other bitch I saw him out with. Banks opened her door and planted a kiss on her cheek before slapping her ass. I cringed watching the scene unfold. My father glanced back at me, disgust evident on his face.

"Is that him?"

"No," I lied but he clearly saw through that shit as he pulled into the driveway. Banks and the woman eyed the car and my father let down my window.

"Why the fuck you poppin' up at my shit? If you bring yo ass back over here again I'mma get a restraining order on yo crazy ass!" Banks ranted.

"Just as I suspected," my father scoffed with a disappointing shake of his head before rolling the window back up. He stepped out of the car and Banks grilled him.

"Who the fuck is you?"

"My name is Pascal Peterson, I'm Shadae's father, and it was brought to my attention that you got my daughter pregnant and she hasn't been able to reach you to discuss what comes next."

"Oooop, on that note, I'm gone. Ion play step mama," the woman standing next to Banks declared.

"Shadae, you better get your pops and get the fuck up off my property with this bullshit. We ain't fucked in like two or three months, ain't no telling who that baby pappy is and yo ass was over here sick and throwing up on New Year's Eve, I hadn't even stuck my dick in you yet. You were pregnant then weren't you? You think I'm dumb? I know how pregnancy works."

Rolling my window back down, I looked up at Banks with fire filled eyes. I planned to remain silent and let my father make a fool of himself in this man's driveway but I refused to let him play me. "I'm seventeen weeks pregnant, ass hole, do the math. I got pregnant the last week of December, first week of January."

"I ain't claiming shit until I get a DNA test. Ion know where else Shadae been, now get the fuck on," Banks retorted.

His tone and choice of words were chilling, leaving me flabbergasted by his reaction. I didn't expect Banks to jump up and express an innate desire to be a family after my announcement but the disrespectful response stung like hell. This man pretended to be a friend, listened to me vent about my parents, their expectations and issues within my relationship with Streetz. Now I realized it wasn't genuine at all. Here my parents were, claiming that anyone else would be better than Streetz, but that wasn't true either. Banks might've come from a decent family, owned a business, and possessed immaculate social skills, but he was a complete asshole underneath it all.

"Get the fuck on!" Banks waved us off and turned to give my father his back.

"Don't disrespect my daughter like that!" My father walked behind Banks but I wouldn't be able to live down another man I was involved with whooping my father's ass. Hopping out of the car, I tugged on my father's arm, pulling him back towards the car with my mother right by my side.

"See dad, I told you not to do this!" I exclaimed, tears cascading down my cheeks. "I didn't need this, I was just fine in my own bubble."

Banks shot me a look of sympathy but he could keep that shit. I just wanted to go home and enjoy some peace and quiet. The outside noise from my parents, the disdain from Banks, the fact that I missed the fuck out of Streetz, and all of the other things I had going on were about to send me into a dark place again. This time I was handling things my way and this was the last time my family would drag me into some bullshit I didn't want to do.

CHAPTER FIFTEEN

Zalana

Stirring from my peaceful slumber, my mind went back to the erotic events from last night and my fluttering eyes popped open. *Was it all a dream?* I wondered to myself as my body shot up in the bed. I spent plenty of nights in my bed waiting impatiently for sleep to consume me but last night, I was knocked out as soon as Tall Man pulled me into his chest.

Slightly hungover, I scanned the room and a familiar cologne wafted through the air. The citrus fruit and other scents that I couldn't place were strong. Tall Man was *really* in this room. I had to pinch myself because I couldn't believe this shit and if my memory served me correctly, the way he licked my pussy and put me to sleep wasn't anything to sneeze at either. His warm tongue turned my yoni out and she was currently thumping, anticipating more.

Tall Man stepped out of the bathroom, his bare chest exposed and a pair of Jordan basketball shorts hanging off his waist. His right hand fumbled around in his hair and I noticed he was taking out his plats. Now that I was sober, I was nervous as shit. My breathing hitched and my palms became sweaty. Not only was Tall Man here, but his rugged handsome face looked even better than I remembered. I gawked at him, unable to think straight as I admired his dark skin that was covered in various tattoos. There wasn't a free space on his arms and the tattoos went up to his exposed neck.

"I'm really in the same room with the man who kidnapped me and I don't even know your name. Tall Man won't cut it anymore so what is your name?"

"If I didn't lick all over your pussy last night I would think you were working for the feds and wearing a wire or some shit," he commented, starting on another plat as he approached the bed where I was seated. "Stop saying that shit though, I *didn't* kidnap you. I happened to be at the wrong place at the wrong time. But what's up, can you help me take my hair out? I'm supposed to get it braided at noon."

"Let me take a quick shower and then I'll help you out. I'll even braid it for you because I'm not ready for you to drop me off just yet," I eased out of the bed.

"Do you even know how to do hair?" Tall Man approached me and gripped my hips, pulling me closer to him.

I experienced his scent up close and personal while admiring the features on his handsome face before I melted into his solid frame. Judge your mammy, because this shit felt good and I didn't want him to free my body from his grasp. This man really had me flustered, I couldn't gather the words to answer his question at the moment. Tall Man's hands wandered upward until he was cupping my chin. I stared into his eyes for a moment while he returned my gaze before our lips collided. I couldn't tell you who initiated the kiss, but I was thankful that it happened. Our tongues danced off of each other, further fueling my yearning for this man whose name I still didn't know.

He gripped the back of my head and deepened the kiss. My body wanted to buckle under the intensity of our connection. I never shared a moment that had me gone like this. This kiss was one that left me feeling a rush of indescribable emotions and sensations; fierce and passionate while simultaneously making me feel romantic and loving. While our bodies connected via the kiss, I felt like time stopped and nothing else mattered. Our initial encounter was a thing of the past while a connection formed between us. He pulled away from me, his dick pressing up against me. The look in his eyes told me that he was conflicted but that kiss provided me more than enough clarity.

Shoving my hands down the front of his basketball shorts, I felt it and bit my bottom lip while taking a deep breath. Just like my imagination portrayed, his dick was long and thick. Pushing him back onto the bed, I couldn't wait to sit on it. He held my waist as I straddled him while gripping the base of his dick.

"Fuck Zalana, you been saving this pussy for me," he uttered as I slid down, suffocating his dick with my walls. I wanted to talk shit but I couldn't, the feeling was sensational and my voice was caught in my throat. He sat up and latched onto my neck while fucking me from below. My yoni leaked for this man like he was her owner and my body betrayed me as well, cumming after only a few strokes and embarrassing me.

"Yeah, this pussy been waiting for me," he commented after the first orgasm ripped through my body and a high pitched moan erupted in his ear. He didn't give a fuck about my pussy convulsing on his dick because he didn't let up his strokes. With one hand, he pulled the shirt over my head and plopped one of my nipples into his mouth as he drilled me in that same position. After a few moments he moved to kissing me again, stifling the moans of pleasure that escaped my lips. This felt intimate, as we were face to face, bodies conjoined by the lips and genitals.

"You still wanna know my name?" He cockily questioned.

"Y... ye... y... yesssss!" My voice jumped with each deep thrust he administered to my center.

"Streetz," he informed me. "Now say that shit when you cum on my dick this time."

I nodded my head rapidly as he took a hold of my neck and applied a light amount of pressure that gradually increased. He licked his thumb and leaned back to give his digit better access to my clit. My body was through and I felt another orgasm approaching. Applying a little more pressure to my neck, I involuntarily met his thrusts because my body was no longer under my control. "Come on Zalana, wet yo dick up. Give me all that shit!" His commanding tone and the sensation from my clit had me screaming his name to the top of my lungs.

"Streetz! Fuck, I'm about to cum, fuck me harder."

"Sayless," he quipped. Gripping my waist he pulled his dick out of me and roughly pushed me down on all fours. Just when I was about to complain about him fucking my nut up he slammed back inside with so much force that I lost the words. Long, deep thrusts had me biting the comforter to muffle my erotic screams. Streetz snatched the covers away and tossed them. "Nah, let me hear it. You told me to fuck you harder!"

"I'm cumming!" He slapped my ass so hard I jumped.

"What I told you to do?"

"Streetz! I'm cumming, Streetz!" I screamed as the everlasting orgasm hit me. Streetz pulled his dick out of me and spilled his seeds on my left ass cheek while he caressed the right one.

Collapsing on the bed, this man had my head in the clouds and I knew it. I dozed off for a moment and woke up when Streetz wiped the warm wet rag across my ass. He carefully cleaned me up and then I felt him easing on top of me. "Zalana, you won't ever get sleep if you naked around me," he notified me. His dick slid into me from behind and I was ready for everything he wanted to give me today.

After that second round of sex I was desperate to find sleep again but Streetz wasn't having that. He pulled me out of the bed and into the shower with him. Now here I was, experiencing the most intimate moment with him. Massaging the conditioner into his scalp, I swear I was falling hard for this man already. "Damn, this shit feels good as fuck," he expressed. "I'mma have to come find you when I need my hair washed. I get to see you naked while you massage my scalp. A nigga can definitely get used to this."

"I can get used to everything about us too."

He went silent and I did the same. Pulling my hands from his scalp, Streetz spun around to rinse the conditioner out of his hair. I scrubbed my body down for the second time with his Dove soap and he took over when he spotted me struggling to reach my lower back. His tongue flicked across my shoulder sending tingles to my yoni.

"You better stop if you want me to braid your hair. You know I have to get back to the girls by three o'clock."

"I'mma chill."

Streetz passed me the rag back and I stepped out of the shower. Drying off with one of his towels, I spotted a two pack of toothbrushes with one missing. Pulling the fresh toothbrush out of the pack, I used it to brush my teeth. When I was done, Streetz turned the water off in the shower and joined me at the sink.

"So you live here now?"

"Temporarily. I ain't know if you was gone have my face all over the news or not so I relocated," he replied. "I told you I ain't have shit to live for and was willing to sit down to do that time but that don't mean I was going to make it easy for them crackas to find me."

"Ughhh, I didn't like it when you said that shit the first time and I definitely don't want to hear you talk like that now. As humans, we tend to overlook the people who are right in our face while focusing on those who don't deserve our attention. I'm sure you have people that love you and want to see you live a prosperous life," I preached. "Plus, I want you around."

"Damn, I ain't gone cap... that shit just hit me hard as fuck. Although my mother has spent her entire life in prison, I still love her and would do anything for her. My mama is what I have to live for. Even without the typical mother figure here for me on a daily basis, I still have her living and breathing. Outside of her, ain't shit else out here for me. Speaking of my mother, I need to write her on JPay because I haven't received a call from her in two weeks and that ain't like her."

Rinsing my toothbrush off, I spun around gripping the sides of his face. "You can add *me* to the list now."

I watched his facial expression, waiting for him to smile, nod in confirmation, or give me any sign that he agreed with me but there was nothing. My heart hurt a little and he must've sensed it because he leaned down, initiating a deep passionate kiss that had my hot ass scooting onto the counter with my legs spread ready for another round of impromptu sex.

"Nah, you just said you gotta be somewhere at three. I need you to throw me two braids in my hair so I can feed you and get you where you need to be. You got me talking too motha fuckin' much."

"Is talking not your thing? You have a sexy ass voice."

"Oh yeah?" he flirted.

"Yeah, you know, I dreamt of running into you on a few different occasions. I never thought those dreams would come to fruition but here I am. Now that I'm here, you kind of forced me to come with you again but I will go anywhere with you. My therapist says it's Stockholm syndrome. But you were very nice and you protected me from the other men. After the way you dicked me down this morning, I know the feelings are very real and you are reciprocating it," I rambled.

"I could only force you anywhere if you weren't prepared," he lifted my chin so we were staring into each other's eyes. "I gave you instructions and you weren't following a single one of them."

"I did follow your instructions," I proclaimed. "I bought a gun and learned how to use it. I even took self defense classes but I couldn't bring my gun and such in the club."

"Take this jewel with you forever. I'd rather be *judged by twelve than carried by six* and Ion slide nowhere without that thang on me. That's why I don't do clubs or a lot of that shit y'all be running to do."

I nodded my head and he pecked my lips. "Come on and do my hair so I can get you where you need to go. Where do you want me to order food from?"

"Whatever is close by and still serving breakfast because I'm starving."

CHAPTER SIXTEEN

Banks

I faced my third blunt since Shadae and her parents left my property and I still couldn't shake that shit they were spitting. My mind was consumed with how a child would change my life. Shadae was about to take my freedom, a portion of my money, and an enormous slice of my sanity. When we initially met, Shadae told me how intrusive her parents were and how that ruined the relationship she had with her nigga in prison.

However, her pops pulling up on me and dropping the news of a pregnancy showed me that the shit was worse than I previously thought. I didn't know if the baby was mine but I knew the chances of Shadae lying and bringing her parents to my house like that were slim. My biggest worry about Shadae carrying my seed was when she got drunk, she couldn't handle her liquor. Vomiting in my dining room and shit on New Year's Eve was the second incident. Taking another pull from my blunt, I thought back to her first incident and really shook my head.

We were at the casino and she was on her third fruity drink watching me play Blackjack. I was up a few bands and I knew that she was bored watching me play because she repeatedly shifted her weight from her left side to right side.

"Here, take this and go play the slots over there or something," I stated, passing her a few hundred dollars.

"I don't know how to play," she replied, distracting me.

"Just stick the money in, pull the lever, and let it do it's thing. Maybe you'll get lucky," I explained, still focused on my own card game.

Shadae eventually stalked off and I glanced over my shoulder to see where she was going. After confirming she was at a slot machine that I could see from here, I refocused my attention on the table. This was the most money I've won in a night and a nigga was feeling good as fuck. My eyes didn't leave the table until my ass started losing. I was up five racks after losing the last three hands so I knew it was time to call it quits and keep the lil cash I had.

Scooping my chips up from the table, I peered at the slot machine that Shadae was previously seated in and somebody's old ass granny on an oxygen machine now occupied the seat. I was probably lost in the game for a good hour so I understood that she probably wanted to switch it up and play some other shit. I called her phone to see where she was at and received her voicemail twice in a row. Mad as a motha fucka, I went to cash in my chips and collect my money before searching the aisle of slot machines for Shadae.

When I decided to give up and head to the elevators I spotted her asleep in one of the chairs at a slot machine. Her head was leaned back, mouth wide open, and she was snoring like a fucking bear. I wanted to leave Shadae's embarrassing ass right there but I thought about my own sister, I wouldn't want a nigga to do Zalana like that so I woke her up and helped her out of the casino. When we got into my truck the tears started.

"I'm so sorry. I know that was embarrassing. That was my first time having alcohol in like six months," she confessed. *"I'm so stressed about my boyfriend getting out next week and I went over my limits."*

"Why is your nigga getting out stressing you?"

"He's in jail because he beat up my dad after my parents talked me into having an abortion. We speak on the phone once a week and he says he still loves me but I'm scared for what things will be like when he gets out, ya know. When he does get out, I'll have to stop hanging out with you and I don't even know if he will want me for real. I'm sorry, now I'm talking too much."

"Nah, you ain't talking too much, this the type of shit you should've been telling me. I can fall back if you wanna focus on that nigga but I'm not about to

play no waitin' games for you to see if that nigga want you. You gotta stand on what the fuck you want, Shadae," I shook my head.

"You've been such a good friend to me and I don't want to lose that."

"Well, I'mma give you some time for your nigga to get out and see what you want but I'm not about to wait around forever."

"Can you give me two weeks to figure my shit out?"

"Yeah you got that," I confirmed.

Shadae relaxed in her seat and I exited the parking garage, headed to her crib. After that day, I gave her space until the deadline arrived. A few hours after I texted Shadae's phone and forced her hand at a decision, she hit me to let me know that her nigga moved out and we picked up like ain't shit ever stop.

Thinking back to that day, I should've left her the fuck alone then but I'd been hanging with Shadae for four months and she never drank when we went out so I thought the first incident was a one time thing. Unfortunately, that wasn't the case. If Shadae knew how to handle her liquor we wouldn't even be having this conversation, I'd be laid up with her like a big happy family.

Calling Zalana back to back, my anger intensified because she agreed to check in while on her trip but I hadn't received a call or text since last night. When I reached Zalana's voicemail for the third time I went to her Instagram account and saw that she was just fine, posting a story of herself in Target shopping. I frantically sent her simple ass a text.

Me: Yo ass was supposed to check in but you can't even do that. I know you straight because I'm stalking yo IG but still. Hit me ASAP. I need to vent.

Grabbing my keys off of the coffee table, I exited my house and went to visit my parents. If Zalana didn't want to hear me vent I had to turn to my parents. Pulling into their driveway my phone vibrated in my cup holder. I snatched it up, hoping that it was Zalana, unfortunately it was my mother. Ignoring her call, I went inside to see what she wanted in person.

"I was just calling you," my mother stated as I entered the home.

"I know ma, but I said I would see what you wanted when I got in here."

She took a large gulp from her wine glass, leaving it empty. My mom closed her eyes for a moment and allowed a few tears to cascade down her cheek. "Do you know where your father is?"

"Nah, I thought he was over here."

"Nope," she huffed, pouring herself a generous amount of wine into the glass. "He isn't answering his phone and the last time he disappeared, something was wrong with Zalana and you all were hiding it from me. Now Zalana is out of town and she's ignoring my calls and your father is missing. I'm having flashbacks, it's giving me PTSD." She jumped out of her chair and lunged at me, snatching a chunk of my shirt with her tiny hands. Out of my entire family, my mama was the smallest. Me and Zalana were both tall. I'm six ten and Zalana was five ten while my mama's lil ass was five two. You couldn't tell her shit though, her height didn't matter, I'd seen her check motha fuckas twice her size. "If something is wrong, you better tell me right now!"

"Ain't nothing wrong with Zalana, ma." I explained, prying her hands off of my shirt. "I was just on her Instagram page and she's turning up having a good time."

"What y'all got going on in here?" My father entered the house, observing our intense interaction. He noticed my mother's tears and frowned his face up at me. "What you did now, Banks?"

"Nothing," I chuckled. "I came over here to chop it up with y'all and mama was freaking out because you and Zalana are ignoring her calls."

"Zenobia, relax baby," my father gently ran his hands down her head then kissed the top of her forehead. "I told you last night I had a meeting and if your ass wasn't always drinking maybe you could remember some shit."

"Fuck you Ezra!" My mom snarled and pulled herself away from him.

I knew how my parents got down and before they started bickering, I decided to drop the news on them because I felt like I was going to explode at any moment. "Shadae is pregnant," I blurted out before wandering into the living room and plopping down on the couch. My hands slid down my face as they trailed me into the room. Hovering over me, they looked on in concern, prompting me to continue. "This girl is about to stress me out and ruin my life."

"Don't be so dramatic, Banks. Shadae has her own money and a career, plus I looked up her family and they are decent folks on paper. She's probably better than any of the other women you've messed around with."

"Shadae looks good on paper but she can't handle her liquor, and I almost had to put her pops on his head a few hours ago for pulling up to my house with that bullshit," I detailed.

"Please don't tell me you did something foolish like deny the child or disrespect Shadae in front of her father," my mom pried, giving me the side eye. Taking a deep breath, I leaned back on the couch, giving my mom the green light to talk shit. "Your silence tells me that you were being an asshole and he matched your energy."

"I'm not about to sit up here and coddle you, Banks." My father started with a disappointed head shake. "I've lectured you on countless occasions about safe sex and the consequences that follow."

"I heard you every time, pops. I use a condom every single time. Now does a condom break here and there? Of course but what am I supposed to do about that?"

"I don't know, maybe purchase a plan b, settle down with one woman so you guys can discuss birth control, or hell get a vasectomy, they are reversible. You had plenty of options but you chose to be reckless and now you have to suffer the consequences."

"Come on pops, you don't even have a vasectomy but you expect me to let somebody snip my balls? Nah, you trippin'. I ain't ready to settle down so I felt like it was best for me not to lead anyone on. Well..." my voice trailed off. "Except for Shadae, I was willing to give shit a real try with her. The vibe between us was cool, I actually enjoyed hanging out with her but I cut her off because I ain't like the way she acts when she get that liquor in her."

"Well, I feel like that's something she can work on." My eyes darted in her direction and I caught myself before I said some shit that got my lips slapped off. It was my mother's drinking that aided in how fast I ran the fuck away from Shadae. The last thing I wanted to do in my late fifties was spend my time wrangling my drunk ass wife like my pops does. "What? She's beautiful, educated, and comes from a good family. I couldn't ask for a better daughter in law. You're twenty-six years old, it won't kill you to slow down," she chirped.

"But what if I don't want to do no shit like that?"

"No matter which route you choose to go, it's time to grow up. I'm going to be a glamma! I can't wait," she squeals. "Banks, send me Shadae's phone number, I'd like to speak with her and her family."

"Naw man, you need to calm down," I shook my head, damn near dizzy from the way this reality check had my head spinning.

CHAPTER SEVENTEEN

Streetz

"Ohhhh, this is my song," Zalana chirped, turning up the radio as I maneuvered through traffic. If she was anyone else I would've told her not to touch my shit or put them out on the side of the road. But it was Zalana and I only had her for a few more minutes so it was her world. She braided my hair, we ate a late brunch, and now I was dropping her off with her homegirls.

"Say that you want me," Zalana started and I already knew she wasn't blessed with a voice. Thankfully, Ashanti sang *Don't Let Them* real chill like because she would've been fuckin' this shit all up. As Zalana sang along to the beat she unbuckled her seatbelt and got into the shit, touching my chin and rubbing her hands down my head the entire time. This girl was so fuckin' extra, on the average day, I despised women who did too much invading my space, but again, this was Zalana. The same chick that ran away from her brother and into a car that wasn't even an Uber.

When Zalana sang that last line she leaned in and pecked my lips while at the red light. I don't know if that was really her song or if it was a covert attempt to express her true feelings for me. Either way, I didn't read minds or play games so I took it for what it was, a terrible car karaoke rendition of the song. Pulling into the driveway of the

Airbnb, I noticed a shift in Zalana's energy before her nonverbal cues followed. In my line of work I mastered the art of reading others. When I threw my car in park Zalana's breathing deepened slightly, her bottom lip poked out, and sadness flooded her eyes. She tore her eyes away from me and observed the other ladies out front pulling Publix bags out of the Sprinter van.

"Let me go see what's going on because it looks like they are unloading."

"Go handle your business," I nodded.

My eyes trailed Zalana until she met Yola in the doorway. They chopped it up for a few and she approached the car with a smile on her face, clearly something cheered her up. "Dro and his brother flew up here so we are staying one more day," she chirped and slid back into the car. "We just need to grab you some swim trunks or something and a bag of ice because they forgot to grab some when they went to Publix. Yola said Dro is cooking on the grill."

I paused for a moment because I didn't do this type of shit. Family gatherings, cookouts, and all of that type of shit was off limits for me. Yeah I knew Dro, we went to the same high school, and I did my own thing on the side, getting my shit from him until he stepped out of the way. The only reason I met his wife was because Dro kept telling me to bring Shadae to Yola's Beauty Lounge and I treated her to a full day there for her birthday. I got back to the salon before Shadae was ready and had to sit in the car and wait for her. Dro pulled up to see his wife and saw my car outside so I got out to greet him. His loud mouth wife came outside talking shit about her food getting cold while he was outside running his mouth. He introduced us and she went on about her business, but I'd seen her regularly after that because Shadae switched to going to Yola exclusively.

"Or did you have something else to do today?" Zalana lamented. "I'm sorry for just assuming."

Real shit, I was supposed to slide back to Tampa to pick up my cash but I didn't want Zalana out of my space just yet. "Nah, we can run by Target real quick."

Zalana perked up and leaned over the seat to assault my face with kisses. When Zalana's lips grazed my philtrum, I felt the sensation on my top lip and smelled her fresh breath at the same time. Gripping the back of her head, I guided her lips down slightly and tongued her down. Without even trying this girl was driving a nigga crazy. "Move Zalana before I sit you on my dick right in this driveway," I commented after breaking the kiss. Zalana bit her bottom lip and I felt like she was challenging a nigga. Shaking my head, I put the car in reverse and backed out of the driveway. Until Zalana left Atlanta, I was down to do whatever she wanted to do as long as her pretty ass was smiling.

Entering Target, I followed Zalana's lead until we made it to the men's apparel section. It quickly became evident that shopping was one of her hobbies because she fumbled through the racks like a pro, pulling out swim trunks, evaluating them, and shoving them back on the rack. A few moments passed and Zalana held up a blue pair with pink, white, and teal hibiscus flowers on them. Shaking my head, I thought about the fact that I didn't own any swim trunks. Although I was born and raised in Florida I wasn't on none of that, pool parties and the beach weren't my thing.

"Naw," I refuted, pushing that shit back on the rack. Back at the house I thought I was willing to do whatever she wanted to do as long as she was happy but that was dead. "I prefer black."

"Come on, please," Zalana poked her lip out and brightened her eyes.

Leaning down, I sucked Zalana's lip into my mouth, swiftly engulfing her into a kiss. Her hands wrapped around my neck and I placed my hands on the small of her back. Someone behind us cleared their throat and I broke the kiss, grabbing the black swim trunks I preferred. I didn't give a fuck about who was trying to squeeze by us in the aisle, I ended the kiss because I was out in public with my guards down and I'd never done that shit until today. Zalana had me out of pocket and that simple gesture brought that realization to the forefront.

"So I take it black must be your favorite color," she questioned, snuggling up against me. I loved the fact that Zalana respected my words the first time and didn't try to argue with my decision.

"Nah, Ion prefer any color over the other. I just like shit to be simple."

"Understood," she nodded. "Can you tell me something else about you?"

"Come on ma, you trying to play 21 questions in the middle of Target? Nah, ask me again when we get in the car," I requested. "Where they keep the ice in here?"

Zalana's phone rang and she answered it. After she ended the call I learned that it was Yola asking for a few additional items, extending our time in the store by another fifteen minutes. We made it back to the cookout a little before five o'clock. Zalana led me to the room she was staying in and we got changed. It took real strength not to fuck her while we changed but I made it through. Joining the party, Zalana fell right in line with her wild ass friends, taking shots, jumping in and out of the pool while dancing and documenting everything for the cameras. I remained off to the side, smoking a blunt while observing the festivities. This was my first time being around a bunch of motha fuckas I didn't know like that since my grandfather's funeral. I didn't enjoy this type of shit for myself but being here was better than being held up in the crib binge watching tv shows or reading books. The fresh air, the laughter from the women, and the smell of the food wafting through the air.

Water dripped off of Zalana's perfect body as she approached me, reaching for her towel. I took a swig from my cup as I watched Zalana dry off with the towel. "Come on, get in with me," she pleaded, plopping down in my lap.

"Nah, I'm good. Y'all have fun, I just like watching you enjoy yourself," I stated.

"Shotttts!" Yola exclaimed, approaching us with a bottle of Hennessy in her hands.

Zalana threw her head back and drank the liquor straight from the bottle. Without skipping a beat, Yola went on to the next chick and Zalana leaned back into my chest. Her damp body moistened mine and I caressed Zalana's back before kissing her lips. "Do you have to be so damn conspicuous?"

Chuckling, she pecked my lips before responding. "Do you have to always be so damn inconspicuous?"

"Y'all make a cute couple," Dro commented, passing by with a tray full of meat in his hands. I ignored that shit and pulled Zalana in for another kiss. Hearing that shit from Dro was just a reminder that we would never be that and for now, I was just happy to make Zalana happy while she was in town.

"Come on so we can make our plates," Zalana pulled me from the chair.

We washed our hands and grabbed plates before making our way around the table that held all of the food. Yola and her sister prepared the sides while Dro and Xan cooked the meat on the grill. Everything looked good as fuck and I wanted a little of everything. Zalana shocked the shit out of me when she piled various food items on her plate. Returning to the backyard, we retreated to the area I was previously seated in.

"I just knew you would stick to the salad or other healthier options on the table based on our previous encounter," I commented as Zalana took a bite out of the ribs.

"No," she chuckled. "I am not a healthy eater at all, I just don't eat fast food. Those places aren't clean enough for me," she replied.

"Understood," I dug into the macaroni and cheese. The space between us fell silent as we ate because everything was good as fuck. Quickly scanning the backyard, I realized everybody was quiet while stuffing their faces, the only sound in the backyard was the music from the Bluetooth speaker.

In the midst of enjoying our meals my phone rang. Using one of the napkins, I cleaned my hands and pulled my phone out of my pocket. It was my Aunt Victoria calling again. Silencing the call, I blocked her ass before sitting my phone on the table. When I got back to the city and found out who gave her my new number, I was breaking my foot off in their ass.

"Is that your girlfriend or something?"

"Fuck no." I kept it brief and was about to finish my food but Zalana's phone started ringing.

Against my wishes, my eyes darted to her phone just as she did

114

with mine. Ion know why I needed to know who the fuck was calling her but I did. Relief spread through me when I viewed the name *Drama Queen* on the screen. Over the months since I last saw Zalana, I did my research on her family to stay abreast of what Redd got me into. Part of my research included adding Zalana on Instagram from a burner account. On a few occasions, I might have gone through her pictures, gawking at all of the photos, and noticed that any pictures that included her mother contained a caption that referred to her as her drama queen.

She glanced at it, hands covered in sauce from the ribs, then turned to me. "Can you please answer it for me? The last thing I need is them panicking and sending the police here. I told them I would be home by now and I forgot to inform them that we were extending our stay."

"Hell naw, is you crazy?" I shook my head.

"I'm not saying you speak to them but answer the call and hold it to my ear, please."

With clarification, I complied and placed the phone up to Zalana's ear. Her coily hair dripped onto my arm while I held the phone in place.

"What the fuck Zalana?!" Her mother screeched into the phone loud enough for me to hear it. Zalana glanced at me, embarrassed as fuck, but I didn't pay her any mind. "We let you go to Atlanta but you can't even follow simple directions and check in and let us know that you're good. How can you expect us to want to give you money to run a business?"

"First, you didn't *let* me go anywhere. I'm grown, ma."

"Zalana don't…"

"Ma, I'm busy and extending my stay, we are leaving in the morning and I'm just fine. I'll call you back when I'm free," Zalana retorted then pulled her head away from the phone. "Can you hang it up for me?"

Ending the call, I placed the phone back down on the table. That call from her mother was confirmation that I didn't need to get into no shit with Zalana. Her parents sounded just as bad as Shadae's people and after the way that ended, I couldn't put myself through that again.

I'm sure I was everything that Zalana's parents never wanted her to bring home.

"You have a thing for helping me huh?" Zalana's question interrupted my thoughts.

"Huh?"

"When my hands were cuffed and you held that blunt to my lips, it was so submissive and now you're holding the phone while I take calls and my hands aren't even cuffed, we've come full circle," Zalana chirped and my eyes darted around, praying nobody heard her.

"You got me fucked up, the only submission between us is when you bend over and submit to this dick. Now stop talkin' about that shit before somebody hears you," I demanded, sliding her cup over to my side of the table. "You had enough to drink for the day too."

"Yes daddy," Zalana cooed, making my dick hard.

"So what type of business your people supposed to be giving you the money for?" I attempted to change the subject to ease my wandering mind.

"Damn, you might really be a lil crazy eavesdropping on my conversations now."

"I couldn't help it, she was so fuckin' loud. Yo parents always treat you like an infant?"

"Sorta kind of," she admitted. "My parents wanted me to go straight to college after high school but I was presented with an opportunity that I couldn't turn down. I went on tour, traveled the world, and met some amazing people but before I could secure my spot in the industry, I suffered an injury that took me out of the game. Then I went through a little depression due to the missed opportunities and when I bounced back and wanted to open up my own dance studio, my parents wouldn't front me the cash. They were still preaching about me going to college and obtaining a degree that I would never use."

"Damn, no wonder I ain't seen you sit the fuck down since we got here."

"Boy hush," she dropped her fork and cleaned her hands. "Dancing is my first love and I'm about to be on a mission to get my shit together to open a studio with or without my parents' assistance."

"This is a party! I know y'all ain't over here talkin' business?" Yola questioned with her hands on her hips.

"Bae, stop minding them people's business and come on. We about to pull out the desserts if y'all want some," Dro pulled Yola towards the house.

"Okay, now that you're all up in my business, I need you to answer my question from earlier and tell me something about you," she offered a smile.

"I love cheesecake and I saw they had one so come on before these drunk motha fuckas eat it all," I expressed and extended my hand to help her out of the chair.

After eating our slices of cheesecake Zalana and the other ladies lined up around the pool while she taught them how to do a TikTok dance while Xan recorded them. I relaxed in the chair and it didn't take long for Dro to make his way over to me.

"Man, when I heard you and Shadae were a thing for real, I just knew y'all would be together forever but clearly I was wrong. How the fuck you end up with Zalana?" Dro pried, plopping down next to me with a blunt in his hand. He extended it in my direction and I waved it off. "Oh, I forgot, this nigga don't smoke shit he didn't roll himself."

"Been that way since I was a jit," I confirmed with a headnod and pulled a blunt that I rolled earlier from behind my ear.

"Ion know how I ended up with Zalana for the weekend but ain't shit serious."

"That's what your mouth say but the way you been droolin' over her all night says otherwise," he noted with a chuckle. I'm sure he was laughing at the fact that I was watching Zalana take shots with the other ladies by the pool. Lighting my own blunt, I leaned back in the pool chair and faced the blunt to help ease the anxiety that rose just thinking about seeing Zalana off tomorrow morning.

I know it might seem like damn, Zalana came along and I was a different person. Opening up to Zalana and attending this pool party that was over capacity in my opinion were only possible because I trusted Zalana. After she held it down and kept my name out of that black and white, I knew Zalana was solid as fuck. That fact alone would make it a million times harder to keep my distance after this weekend.

CHAPTER EIGHTEEN

Zalana

*A*round ten o'clock Streetz let me know that he was ready to take it in. I had enough food, liquor, and fun so I snuggled up next to him, waved goodbye to the ladies, and exited with him. When we got back to his place we showered together but Streetz didn't touch me like I expected him to. Slipping into the bed, I quickly realized why his behavior switched up since we left the cookout.

"We gotta dead whatever this is we got going on after tonight, you know that right?" Streetz question as I slipped my legs under the covers.

His words caught me off guard and I froze up for a brief moment. I felt comfortable with him, I enjoyed his company and needed to know more about him, but Streetz clearly had a different idea about what was transpiring between us. After spending the day with him in front of others I didn't feel like we came off as anything but a pair that met and were exploring things with each other. The urge to express those feelings rose with each passing second but I remained silent. I understood where Streetz was coming from. If our secret ever came out, my parents would do everything within their power to ensure that he was incarcerated for the rest of his life. Then they would probably banish me to a mental institution for dealing with him. Taking a deep breath,

I silently laid down with my back to Streetz. There wasn't anything else to say because he was right.

"Come on Zalana, don't be like that," he leaned over and planted a kiss on my cheek.

"I'm not trying to be like anything," I rolled over onto my back and gave him my attention. "I understand where you are coming from and I agree. I don't like it but I understand."

Streetz collapsed on the bed next to me and pulled me into his chest. We fell asleep in that position and I got the best sleep in his arms. The next morning I only had enough time to handle my hygiene and eat breakfast that Streetz cooked before he had to drop me off with the ladies.

"Make sure you remember that shit I told you. Be more aware of your surroundings and keep that thang on you," Streetz voiced as we rolled my luggage outside.

"Oh Lord, he's worse than Dro. The nigga gone swear he yo daddy, run girl," Yola quipped before climbing onto the Sprinter van.

Streetz shook his head and dapped Dro and Xan up while waving at Anya as she piled onto the Sprinter van. The other ladies flew home since Dro and Xan were here now. They refused to let me fly home because they promised Banks that they would return me in one piece. The only reason I didn't argue with them was because the flights left early this morning and I would've lost time with Streetz. I hugged and kissed Streetz like he was getting ready to turn himself into the feds before climbing on the Sprinter van and heading back to Tampa.

"Remember what I said and be safe," he repeated himself now that we were the only ones outside.

"I will remember. Take care of yourself," I kissed him again before finally breaking away from him.

Prior to leaving for Atlanta, I was living with my parents but I lost a small piece of my heart and I wanted to be alone. The ladies dropped me off at home and I went inside to get my feelings together. I felt terrible because my parents called a few times after I didn't come back to their house as scheduled but I was ready to regain my independence.

Pushing my suitcase up against the wall, I maneuvered through my home for the first time in months. I was thankful that Banks or my father came to take out the trash but the place still held a stale odor because my wall flowers were empty. Wrangling my curls up into a high bun, I kicked off my shoes and pulled the refills out of the linen closet and went around the house replacing them. Then I went into the kitchen and tossed all of the food from the refrigerator into the trash can. Today, I was taking my life back, the trip to Atlanta and my time with Streetz showed me that I needed that.

My car was still at my parents' house and I refused to ever take an Uber again so I placed an Instacart order to replenish my refrigerator. After changing my sheets and taking a shower, the groceries arrived and I finally decided to respond in the family group chat.

Me: I made it back from Atlanta but I decided that I'm moving back home. This trip pulled me back out of my shell and I need my independence back. I love you guys. Banks, I'm cooking lasagna so I'm positive that I'll see you whenever you come home.

Drama Queen: Zalana! Why didn't you speak with us about this decision before making the move? We wanted additional security measures in place before you went home.

Banks: I been over here waiting for your ass but you know I'mma slide through for that lasagna tonight. Put extra pepperonis on that for me.

Daddy: I won't argue with you Zalana. If you are staying there tonight, Banks needs to stay with you or you need to go to Banks' house. Your mom wanted these motion sensors added to all of your entrances and windows but we haven't gotten around to installing them.

Drama Queen: And you better get on that tomorrow! I asked you to do it two months ago.

Daddy: (exhaling emoji)

Drama Queen: (eye rolling emoji)

I read their messages but didn't reply because there wasn't anything anyone could say to change my mind. Tonight I was going to cook lasagna, sip on my wine, and dive deep into my damn feelings. While cooking I put on my Ashanti playlist and skipped straight to *Don't Let*

Them then sang my mangled heart out over the ground beef and boiling noodles. When the lasagna was done I ate a small plate with a glass of pinot noir then went to take a shower. While the water cascaded down my body, I had a strong urge to call my therapist to tell her what happened but then I had to check myself. She definitely would have attempted to convince me to turn him into the police.

In the middle of massaging the Fenty overnight recovery cream into my skin, my phone chimed with an alert from the security system. A clip of Banks entering my home played on the screen. At least now the new security system will let me know when his creep ass was in my shit without my permission. Descending the stairs about twenty minutes later in my robe and fuzzy slippers, Banks was on the phone, allowing me to catch the tail end of a heated debate.

"Look, I'm trying to do right and you're being difficult as a motha fucka, what's up?" He paused for a moment then looked down at his phone. "Stupid ass girl hung up on me," he mumbled to himself.

"Well not only are you in my shit, but you're bringing negativity and drama with you. I'm changing my code tomorrow to keep you out. It's time to set some boundaries."

"Nah, you can't do me like that right now. I'm in a crisis situation," Banks exhaled deeply before shoving a forkful of lasagna into his mouth.

"And another thing, can you at least eat at the table or the breakfast bar?" I snatched his plate and went into the dining room.

"Why you tripping? Wassup, is there something in the water? You trippin', mom trippin' and..." Banks' voice trailed off before he plopped down into one of my chairs. "I done fucked up for real this time and that's why I've been calling you. Shadae is pregnant."

I gasped and took the seat next to him. "For real?"

"Mannnnnnnnn," he exhaled. "I wish I was bullshitting. Now ma went and met Shadae and her mother for lunch today and been on my head talking about how nice she is and that I should really consider settling down."

"Now why did you give mama that girl's phone number, you knew she was gone do the most."

"That's the thing, I didn't give her shit. She found Shadae on Facebook and inboxed her. After Shadae didn't reply to her message all day yesterday, ma found the girl's mama and inboxed her and that's how they all ended up at lunch together today. Shadae trippin' out on me like I set the shit up or something. But yo mama be trippin' for real man, who does that?"

"Zenobia, she don't have anything else to do," I chuckled, pouring myself a glass of wine. "I know you fucked up right now but I can't wait to be an aunty," I held my glass of wine up and did a lil twerk with my tongue out.

"Man hell naw, this why I don't need no daughter. Between you and mama, Ion know which one of y'all would be the worst influence on a lil girl," he shook his head.

"I'm going to be a great influence," I affirmed. "Plus Shadae is beautiful and I hope that you have a beautiful dark skinned baby because her complexion and skin are everything. Lord, please give Banks a lil girl that I can spoil and I'll have a best friend forever."

Banks ran his hands down his face and pulled them into the prayer position. The stress was evident but shit, Shadae was better than a lot of the other hoes he fucked on. I gently rubbed his shoulder while mentally preparing some kind words. To be honest, I really didn't know what to say to Banks. He was sitting up here distraught about a situation that could've been avoided. I swear my daddy gave him the safe sex talk so often that it used to piss me off. Yet here he was, distraught because he had a baby on the way. A forceful knock appeared at the door and I was thankful for the interruption. Standing from my chair, I looked around for my phone so I could check the security cameras but realized I left it upstairs. Figuring that I would check the peephole, I headed for the door.

"Man sit yo ass down, I got it," Banks announced.

I followed his request because I wasn't expecting anyone. Banks checked the peephole then opened the door.

"Who the fuck is you and what the fuck you want?"

"Ain't no pressure, I got something for Zalana. Make sure she gets it," Streetz's voice caused the hairs on the back of my neck to stand up and my yoni to throb simultaneously. At that moment, I guess I could understand where Streetz was coming from when he said we couldn't be together because this shit was terrifying. At the same time, I couldn't help the way my heart yearned for his touch, smell, presence, hell everything about him. After shaking the sense of panic, I rushed over to the door just as Banks was closing it.

"Streetz!" I yelled his name, jogging behind him. My fuzzy slippers didn't stop until I tugged on his arm to cease his stride. "That's not some dude I'm dealing with, that's my brother Banks," I clarified once he gave me his attention.

"I know, clearly I did my research on you and your family after I left you at the fire station. How do you think I knew where to pull up on you at?"

"Makes sense," I nodded.

"I gotta slide, I just wanted to drop a gift off to you real quick."

"Okay, ummmm... Are you in town to stay?" I wondered.

"I believe I am," he smiled then planted a kiss on my cheek. I'm sure Banks was watching but I didn't give a fuck. Gripping Streetz's chin, I pulled him in and initiated a nasty kiss. If Streetz wouldn't have pulled away, I would've kept him there all night.

"Come on man, your brother already look like he wanna off a nigga," Streetz shook his head.

"See you around Zalana."

"See you around."

I remained in that position, eyes glued to Streetz's car until he turned the corner.

"Who the fuck is that nigga and why he left you so much money?" Banks grilled me, thumbing through the stacks of money he pulled out of the manilla envelope.

"I don't know but give it here!" I snatched my money and the envelope away from him.

Scanning the envelope there was a small note inside. Sliding it out, I wished that I was alone so I could've smelled it to see if it carried Streetz's scent. Fighting my quirky actions, I read the note to myself, *For your dance studio.* Closing my eyes, I took a deep breath and placed the card over my heart. A lone tear escaped my eyes because I was emotional as fuck, I was one step closer to fulfilling my lifelong dream thanks to Streetz. At that moment, I realized that I didn't give a fuck about anything anyone could say about a relationship forming between us. I wanted to run to him, embrace his strong body with a hug then wrap my lips around his dick and never let him go, but I didn't even know how to get in touch with him.

"What the fuck is you crying for?" Banks interrupted my moment and snatched the card away from me.

"Ah hell naw! I ain't never seen you with that nigga before so you don't need to take money from him, he doesn't have to give you shit. I was going to surprise you with the money to open your studio, I had this surprise in the works for you since January second before all of the crazy shit went down. I figured I would surprise you when you were ready to step back into the world after everything that happened."

"Okay Banks, give me the money and I'll give Streetz his money back."

"Bet, he ruined my surprise but Ion want you taking shit like that from no nigga," Banks continued.

"See, I'm glad you got Shadae pregnant, maybe now you can get out of my business and stop acting like my damn daddy and focus on your own child," I mushed his head.

"Nah, never that."

I really wasn't giving anybody shit back but I would gladly accept double the money if they were offering it. Banks continued talking shit while I sat on the couch but I tuned him out, the only thing on my mind was how the fuck I could get in touch with Streetz.

CHAPTER NINETEEN

Banks

Four Weeks Later
May 2022

$\mathcal{M}$y life was changing and everything was moving too fuckin' fast and I could be honest and say that I wasn't prepared for none of this shit. A child, another human that would depend on me and a baby mama that didn't know how to handle her liquor. Sitting back on my roof facing a blunt, I couldn't believe that this was real life. My phone vibrated and it was Rue calling. I been ignoring my niggas' calls and texts since Shadae dropped this bomb on me because I ain't want to talk about this shit anymore. My phone alerted me to motion at my front door and I opened the livestream to see Rue and Zaire standing on my doorstep talking shit.

"Something better really be wrong. Got us looking for his ass like we his bitch or something. The lil bih who works in his shop that I be knocking down said he hasn't been to the dispensary or answering their calls. Everything been going through his assistant manager," Zaire told this nigga my business.

They started knocking again and I opened the app to unlock the door from my phone. After hearing the automatic click, they entered my crib and headed straight for the roof. I loved these niggas, they were my boys since middle school and they were always at my crib growing up to help me cope with being in a house with my mother and sister majority of the time while my father was working. Their actions didn't surprise me because a few years ago, Rue and Cici suffered a miscarriage and he went off the grid. After not hearing from him and being ignored by Cici as well, we pulled up to make sure they were straight. That was the type of bond we had, they were my brothers and I'd have their backs until the caskets dropped.

"What the fuck wrong with you? Why you over here ignoring everybody? You ain't been to the dispensary and you had us worried," Rue questioned, plopping down next to me.

Exhaling deeply, I wasted no time coming out with my issues because I had shit to do. "I fucked around and got Shadae pregnant."

"The drunk bitch whose cousin had to pick her up from your crib on New Year's Eve?" Zaire inquired.

"Yeah man."

"I thought you said you were leaving her alone after that night."

"Clearly I backslid a time or two. The pussy was good and the head was superb," I shrugged.

"At least yo baby mama got some good pussy," Rue laughed. "You over here high and sulking like it's the end of the fuckin' world. You havin' a jit right on time because the baby gone be right behind my twins so they will grow up together."

"Mannnnn, I ain't trying to be holding babies in carriers and pushing strollers and shit. That's gone scare the hoes off. Her parents pulled up on me hollin' bout she was pregnant when I was walking Mari's thick ass to the car. She ain't answered the phone for me since, said she don't play step mama before she swerved off though."

"Cheer up nigga. You gone still get hoes, have time to chill and shit, but you will have a little human that loves you unconditionally when it's all said and done. I just pray your baby mama don't be causing you hell when the baby comes, everything else is going to be straight. Tonight we gone grab drinks to celebrate my boy about to be somebody's pappy," Rue lectured.

"Yeah, just let me know where because I gotta go grab Shadae and take her to her doctor's appointment in a few. My mama been on my ass talking about I need to be at every appointment and shit. She even called an interior decorator over here to get some ideas together for a nursery like they gone be staying over here. Zenobia think she slick because every time we talk, she bring up me and Shadae being a beautiful family and all that shit."

"Ion even wanna think about Margaret putting that type of pressure on me," Zaire commented, referring to his mother. "This was a big reminder for me to wrap my dick up and keep the Plan B on deck, these hoes gotta take it before they leave the crib if we have an incident."

"That's probably how Shadae got me," I confessed. "I always strapped up but when we had an incident and needed a Plan B, I didn't watch her take the shit. I just had it delivered to her house."

"And that's where you fucked up. You know you a lick."

"Man fuck all that, shit just pushing my mind into deeper darker holes," I stated. Unlocking my phone, I clicked around until I pulled up a short clip of that nigga who gave Zalana all that money. Zalana wasn't slick, I knew she didn't give that nigga his money back but I still wanted to give her the cash for her dance studio because I didn't want him to be able to say my sister needed him for shit. "Y'all know this nigga?"

They both observed the video a few times before responding with an unanimous no.

"Who is he?" Zaire inquired.

"Ion know but he clearly sniffing behind my sister. Came over here and dropped fifty bands on her then left. She being secretive as fuck about it too. Said it wasn't anything like that ... he just wanted to invest in her like I'm a blind dummy that didn't see them kissing," I grumbled as my phone went off. It was a call from Shadae and I quickly answered before they could respond.

"Wassup."

"Hey, I just wanted to check to see if you were still coming to pick me up and take me to the doctor's appointment."

"Yeah, I'm leaving my crib now," I informed her.

"Okay. I'll see you soon."

Ending the call, I ushered the fellas out of my crib and drove across town to Shadae's house. When she got in the car the shit was awkward and silent but I didn't mind because my mind was all over the place. When we arrived at the gynecologist office I followed Shadae's lead because this shit wasn't my lane. Shadae was sent to the bathroom when we first arrived and she told me to take a seat in a second lobby until she came back. After a few minutes in the second lobby, we were seated in an exam room where she sat on a table. When the doctor came into the room, my attention was on the monitor as a grainy black and white ultrasound image was displayed.

"Let's take a listen to the baby's heart," the doctor stated before clicking around on his device. The rapid thumbs filled the room and something in me flipped. For the first time, I felt a connection to the baby and a protective nature for Shadae and my unborn child came over me. Standing from my chair, I walked over to the bed and stood closer to Shadae, gaining a better view of the image. "Would you guys like some pictures to take home?"

"Yeah, two copies of each please," I requested.

Looking at Shadae, I sensed that she was more at ease with me closer to her. As the doctor printed off the images I debated on whether or not holding her hand to show my support would make things awkward or lead her on in any way. Shoving my runaway thoughts to the back of my mind, I gripped Shadae's hand and offered her a reassuring smile. "I got y'all." She grinned and nodded her head in understanding then the room fell silent again.

Shadae handled the checkout process and we conferred about her next appointment so I could be present. On the ride home, I broke the silence in an attempt to clear the air between us. "I uhhh... I want to apologize for the way I reacted the day I found out you were pregnant. You, your parents, and the news all caught me off guard."

"I understand," Shadae lamented. "I know that my behavior when I drank around you was atrocious so I completely understand you wanting to end things between us. Your mom brought my previous drunken antics up to my parents and I haven't heard the end of it since then. I'm not mad but I just want to assure you that I won't be touching alcohol while I'm pregnant and probably never after either. I was going through a lot."

"Shit, I'm glad to hear that," I nodded. "If I'm being honest, that shit is my biggest concern. I want you to be the best mother to our child and I'm going to match your energy and be there every step of the way. I'm also here if you need a listening ear, we were friends before we crossed that line."

"Do you really want to hear about my issues?"

"Lay it on me."

"After the abortion and altercation that led to Streetz's incarceration, I fell into a deep depression. I didn't have the man I thought was my soulmate or my baby and I was alone. That led to me drinking and the occasional drink became a daily thing. I'm happy that I caught myself and got my shit together because I got to the point that I was sipping wine between my classes and doing a lot of shit that I regret."

"Damn, you can't let shit eat you up like that."

"I know, I'm in therapy now and I don't see myself drinking ever again. Not even wine, I didn't like who I was when I got drunk. To be honest, I was prepared to raise this baby alone. I took my time to formulate a plan and was going to execute it without bothering anyone but here we are now. My parents are a lot and clearly your parents are as well but I mean this from the bottom of my heart, you can go on about your business after today. I don't need the negativity around me and I won't force anyone to do anything they don't want to do."

"Stop that shit," I shook my head. "I'm here and we gone do this."

Shadae smiled at me and that shit warmed my heart a little. Maybe her ass would grow on me and we would take things back out of the friendzone, only time would tell. For now, I wanted to support her with anything she needed throughout this pregnancy.

"Aye," I interrupted the silence in the truck.

"Yeah?"

"Yo people are a lot and my mama is a lot but we not about to be doing a bunch of bullshit just because they want us to. I'mma check yo parents just like I would check mine. You have to grow a backbone baby girl because Ion need you doing no bullshit then coming back to me talking about your parents talked you into doing it. Think for yourself and stand firm on your own feelings and boundaries, even with them."

"I know," she took a deep breath. "I promise I'm working on it but that's easier said than done."

"So when do we find out what we having?"

"Whenever you want to. I planned to wait until the baby came to be surprised."

"Nah, if that's how you planned to do shit, we can keep it like that. You want a girl or a boy?"

"I'm going to be happy either way as long as the baby is healthy and as you heard, he or she is growing strong," Shadae smiled and rubbed her stomach that was barely there. If you didn't know her you would've thought she was just full but pre-pregnancy Shadae had a washboard flat stomach and she loved to show that shit off.

"I ain't gone cap, I'm hoping for a boy. I'mma love jit either way, but I want a junior that I can keep on my side," I grinned.

"I bet," Shadae nodded her head and looked out the window as we pulled into her driveway.

"You hungry?"

"No, I just want to go lay down."

"Alright, make sure you eat and get a lot of rest and hit me if you need anything."

"Thank you, Banks," Shadae expressed before exiting the truck. I sat there until she made it safely inside and took off.

The next stop was my dispensary since they were out here telling people I was missing, I wanted to show my face. Before I could make it there, I received a text message from Rue that made me bust a U-turn and head towards Hillsborough Avenue where her studio was located. It was a screenshot from the Hillsborough County Sheriff's office with a mugshot for the nigga who left Zalana all of that money. *Samuel Johnson AKA Streetz.* He was arrested for a bunch of shit about a year and a half ago and spent a year in prison. Thinking back, I knew I heard Zalana call him something but I couldn't quite make it out. It definitely could have been Streetz.

Four weeks lapsed since that nigga popped up at Zalana's crib and I hadn't seen him return but I needed to make sure my sister was steering clear of that nigga. In the month since I gave Zalana the money for her studio, she put in the work to bring her dreams to fruition. Pulling up to the space she rented and turned into her own spot, I was proud as fuck of my sister for making her dreams come true. Our parents didn't even know about this spot yet. Zalana said the dance studio was special to her and she didn't want them throwing negativity her way. Thinking about that almost made me pause before I entered her spot talking shit but I couldn't hold back.

"Wassup bruh," I greeted the man who was putting the logo on her glass door.

Entering her spot, it was a pink heaven. The walls were hot pink, the chairs were light pink, and everything else in the studio was a different shade of pink. Zalana was across the studio wiping down the glass mirror that covered the entire back wall. She spun around when she saw me and her facial expression went from jovial to confused when she saw my mug.

"What's wrong with you?"

"How you know this nigga?" I interrogated, flashing the nigga's mugshot in her face.

"Oh my God, Banks, why are you looking into him? I haven't even talked to him since that day. How I know him isn't your business so can you mind your own?"

"It is my business when you receiving large sums of money from the nigga. I knew something was up because that money was rubber banded up, they ain't come from no fuckin' bank. Is you into some bullshit Zalana with that nigga? You moving drugs for him? I always thought it was suspicious that they couldn't connect the Lucero Mafia to your kidnapping. Did that shit really have something to do with that nigga and they were using that as a cover?"

Zalana tensed up for a millisecond but I caught that shit. I knew my sister better than anyone else walking the face of this earth and something was off. I struck a nerve with that shit. "Oh my God, Banks, what is wrong with you? How could you accuse me of some shit like that?"

"Save that bullshit Zalana and tell me what the fuck is up."

"Get the fuck out, Banks! I don't come to your place of business causing a scene so please give me the same respect."

"Fuck that, I gave you the money for this so I'mma act however the fuck I want to around this bitch. Especially when it's in regards to you and your safety now stop playing with me, Zalana. What you got going on with that nigga?" I roared.

Zalana looked away for a moment and then stared me down with furious eyes. "I met him in Atlanta, we fucked, and he wanted to give me some money. I don't have his phone number, I didn't know his real name until a few seconds ago when you shoved his mugshot in my face, and I haven't spoken to him since the day he popped up at my place. It's an ugly truth and I hope you are satisfied now."

Disgusted, I didn't half believe Zalana's ass because I never even saw her bring a nigga back to her spot and trust me, my nosey ass was waiting for the day so I could run the nigga off. Whether it was true or not, it was still a lot for me to hear Zalana say that shit. Turning around, I exited the studio before the man working on her door heard anymore of our business. I wasn't satisfied with Zalana's answers so I was going to bring that shit to pops' attention. He had more resources to look into the nigga than I did.

CHAPTER TWENTY

Zalana

anks flipped my attitude from sugar to shit in a matter of seconds. I was on a high, happy that my studio was coming together beautifully, and the social media ads were bringing in a slew of inquiries. My website was up and I already had a handful of girls signed up and ready to start this summer session just a few weeks away.

Everything was falling into place but I still have a few items on my to-do list. I wanted some time to hire an assistant instructor to help the ladies who were struggling to catch on or fill in for me if I ever needed to take time off. Then I needed to think of a cute name for my girls. I wanted some shit that popped out when we went to competitions. Excitement surged through me as I daydreamed about my future achievements. The high that I was experiencing wiping down the windows that the contractor hung up before moving to place the decals on my door felt better than smoking on a fat blunt.

Then here Banks came, fucking up my mood and putting my mind back on Streetz when I tried so hard not to think about him. I searched for him on Facebook, Instagram, and Twitter but couldn't find him on any social media platforms. After wiping down the mirrors I remembered the name under Streetz's mugshot so I went to look him up. The fact that Streetz had a mugshot didn't surprise me, it was clear from the manner in which we met that he was into illegal shit.

"I'm all done with the front door so I'm about to head out. We appreciate you for entrusting us with your business. When I get home, I'm going to email you a coupon for fifteen percent off any future service."

His voice caused me to jump because my back faced the door as I was going through Streetz's criminal history. I was so engrossed in this man's business that I didn't hear the contractor sneak up behind me. That forced me to think about Streetz even harder, I wasn't aware of my surroundings like he continuously preached. "Ms. Moore, are you okay?"

"Yeah, I'm sorry. I have a lot on my mind," I offered him a faint smile. "I'm going to send a tip via Zelle for your hard work. I truly appreciate you."

"You're welcome. Have a good night and make sure you lock this door behind me."

"I'm leaving right behind you," I announced, snatching my purse off of the table.

Trailing the contractor out of the studio, I locked up and decided to act on a plan that I executed mentally over a thousand times since I last saw Streetz but was always too terrified to make it a reality. Pulling out of my assigned parking spot, I also made a mental note to give Banks his money back tomorrow. He wanted to throw up what he did for me as an excuse to cause a scene in my place of business. While Banks was worried about Streetz being able to claim that he bankrolled my business, he was doing the same thing. In my opinion it was deplorable coming from Banks because he was my brother.

Shoving my current disdain for Banks to the back of my mind, I maneuvered through traffic until I arrived at Yo's Beauty Lounge. It was the middle of the afternoon on a Wednesday and that showed in the parking lot because there was only one car outside. Entering the shop, I quickly got hot from nervousness but gained a confidence boost when I saw that Yola was in the shop by herself.

"Ion know how many times I'm gone have to tell these heffas to lock that door when we close up for lunch," Yola rolled her eyes before greeting me. "Thank God it's you but we are closed because everybody went to lunch and Dro is on his way up here to take me to lunch," Yola spoke before embracing me with a hug.

"I'm not here for any services today. I was actually hoping to run into Dro when I got here."

"Huh?" Yola puzzled, quickly cocking her head to the side.

"Oh no, not like that," I corrected with a nervous chuckle. "Hell, asking you might be better. Do you think you can get some information about Streetz from Dro for me?"

"You was ducked off with that nigga while we were in Atlanta and didn't get his phone number? That ain't how the game goes, Zalana. You not supposed to be chasing niggas, they supposed to chase you."

"I know and usually, I wouldn't do this but our situation is complicated."

"It ain't my business but unless you pregnant, there ain't any other complication that should lead you to hunt a nigga down."

"I just want to tell him thank you. He popped up at my house when we got back from Atlanta and dropped off the money for me to open my dance studio like I always dreamed of and have a little money left over. I haven't seen him since then and I want to invite him to my grand opening and say thank you. That's all," I pleaded.

"Bitch, you trying to get my head knocked between the washer and the dryer asking my husband about another nigga but you can stick around the shop until Dro gets here and ask him yourself. I'm already in enough trouble because my mama's talking ass told Dro about the stripper pole lesson you gave me. I posted it on my Instagram stories and she went running that fat ass mouth. I had to kick her ass out of my Close Friends for that shit."

"I'm so glad my parents don't know how to work Instagram. My mom will stalk the fuck out of your Facebook but she don't know anything about Instagram," I chuckled as the door opened up.

I tensed up once I saw Dro. The moment was here and now I was choking up.

"I thought you said you were free to go to lunch?" Dro questioned Yola.

"I am, Zalana is here to talk to you."

135

"About what?" Dro glanced my way.

"Ummm, I was hoping that you could give me Streetz's phone number."

"You trippin', I can't give you that man's number. Ion give out people's info and even if I did, Streetz ain't the type of person you can give his shit out unless you have permission."

"Come on and help my girl a lil, Dro. Just call Streetz and ask for permission and if he say no then that's it."

"I'll call him but if he don't answer, you gone have to find another way to get at that man."

"I can accept that," I nodded my head.

Dro initiated a call to Streetz and I held my breath while he stood next to Yola in silence.

"Wassup jit," Dro spoke into the phone and my heart beat rapidly while I impatiently waited for him to get through the pleasantries and ask the damn question. "Ain't shit, I just slid on my wife to take her to lunch and the lil Zalana chick up here asking for your number." Dro paused for a moment and the look he flashed my way told me that Streetz refuted my request. "Alright." Dro replied.

Without thinking, I snatched the phone away from him and placed the phone to my ear. "Streetz please meet me somewhere. If you're in Atlanta I can fly up there to meet you," I pleaded. Glancing at Dro, I knew that I looked desperate and prayed he would forgive me for invading his personal space.

"I'm not far from the shop so chill out until I get there."

Streetz ended the call and I passed Dro his phone back. "I'm sorry about that."

"You straight," he laughed. "If you knew the shit I pulled when I first met Yola, you'd know you don't have shit on me."

"And his ass isn't exaggerating either," Yola cooed.

"I'm going to grab my purse."

"Chill out, we waiting for Streetz to come get Zalana," Dro informed her. "If her impatient ass would've given me half a second, I could've told her that."

Embarrassed, I claimed a seat and Streetz arrived less than five minutes later. He entered the shop dressed casually in a pair of basketball shorts and a black t-shirt just like every other time we saw each other.

"I know y'all about to have a cute lil reunion and everything but I'm hungry so you don't have to go home but you have to get the hell up out of here," Yola jested, walking over to grab her purse.

I strutted over to Streetz, wishing I got dressed before coming here because I was wearing a pair of joggers and an oversized t-shirt. When I was within arm's length, he pulled me in for a hug and that familiar scent hit me immediately, leaving me mesmerized.

"Where y'all about to eat at? We gone slide with y'all," Streetz questioned Dro.

"Oh my God, no, we weren't going to lunch for real. We trying to do freaky shit but Zalana popped up and now you over here too. I'd suggest y'all hit Another Broken Egg, have some food and mimosas, and find somewhere to do what we tryin' to do. Now shoo," Yola ranted, pushing us towards the exit. I was laughing at her silly ass as we approached my car until the door to the Denali parked a few spaces down opened and we came face to face with Banks.

"B... B... B... Banks, what are you d... doing here?" I stuttered, my jovial appearance washed away with a horrified expression.

"You said you didn't have this nigga's number and you haven't spoke to him since the day he popped up at your crib, but you run yo ass straight to him after we get into it? This is why I'm always up in your business, you don't make good decisions. This ain't the type of nigga you gone be fucked up with," Banks ranted.

"Ion wanna have to put you on yo ass since you Zalana's brother but watch yo tone when you speaking to her," Streetz monotoned.

"With all due disrespect, fuck you. I'mma talk to my sister however the fuck I wanna. Come on Zalana, we can talk about this shit back at the crib," Banks spat and roughly tugged on my arm.

I dug my heels into the ground and pulled away from him because he clearly lost his damn mind. Even daddy didn't handle me like that. The vice grip Banks had on my wrist didn't budge, forcing me to yell. "Get off of me, Banks! What the fuck is wrong with..."

Before I could finish my sentence, Streetz punched Banks in his face. This shit went from terrible to atrocious as they exchanged blows, falling from the hood of my Benz to the side of Banks' Denali. These two were going so hard that my Benz now had a huge dent on the hood. They were both on the taller side but Banks had Streetz by at least four or five inches in height. Size didn't matter because Streetz found a way to get Banks in a headlock and I noticed his busted lip.

"Streetz, please let him go!" I pleaded, gently tugging on his arm that was wrapped around Banks' neck.

"If it wasn't for the same woman you were just disrespecting a few minutes ago, I would end yo dumb ass."

"What the fuck is you niggas doing?" Dro shouted upon exiting the beauty lounge. He jogged over in our direction where I was trying to pry Streetz off of Banks. "Come on Streetz, not in front of my wife's shit."

Streetz released the grip he had on Banks, allowing his body to tumble to the ground. Banks desperately accepted oxygen into his lungs and I dropped down beside him to make sure he was fine.

"See the type of nigga you bringing around! You so fuckin' stupid I swear." Banks struggled to chastise me as he stood up.

I looked up and Streetz was on the way to his car but spun around at the sound of Banks' voice. "I told yo ass not to talk sideways to her."

"Chill Streetz!" Dro sounded off as he marched in our direction.

"I ain't on that, he see I ain't shit to fuck with. That weight don't mean shit over here," Streetz spat. "Come on Zalana," he extended his hand in my direction. I rolled my eyes at Banks and accepted Streetz's embrace. "I'm about to take your sister on a trip to apologize for beating yo ass. You better hope Ion bring her back pregnant, brother-in-law," he spat.

"Whew shit nah," Yola finally spoke, fanning herself at Streetz's words. I was happy for her outward expression because that's exactly how I felt on the inside as he opened the passenger door to his car for me to slide inside.

"Clearly you wasn't watching your surroundings if your brother followed you over here without your knowledge," Streetz calmly broke the silence as we hopped on the interstate. I noticed his eyes looking in the rearview mirror.

"That's exactly why I need you around," I flirted to break the awkward silence. Streetz reached over and gripped my hand then brought it to his lips.

"Where are we going? If you meant what you said about taking me on a trip, I need you to go home and pack a bag first and my home is in the opposite direction."

"Nah, I got you."

His words were soothing and I believed every syllable he uttered. Relaxing in the seat with Streetz's hand locked into mine, I was prepared to end up wherever he took me.

CHAPTER TWENTY-ONE

Banks

"*Y*ou straight bruh?" Dro questioned while I heaved over, attempting to catch my breath.

I didn't respond before stalking off because I was liable to spaz on Dro and have to fight him next. Everything about that interaction caught me off guard. From Streetz punching me in my face to Zalana leaving with that nigga. As bad as I wanted to go tell my pops what was going on, I didn't. He would do some wild shit like have the police looking for that nigga while Zalana was in the car with him and that could turn the situation worse. My eye was throbbing as I slid into the car and I felt it swelling shut.

Maneuvering through traffic, I went to Shadae's house because she lived the closest and my eye was throbbing. The more time moved my throat started burning as well, it felt like my shit was on fire. I used my free hand to rub my neck while stretching it in search of relief. Pulling into Shadae's driveway, I spotted her seated on the porch talking on the phone. Her face frowned up as she approached my car and I killed the engine. Suddenly, I had second thoughts about letting Shadae see me like this but she pulled my door open, ready to talk shit about my presence until she saw my face. The annoyed glare morphed into a concerned expression.

"Let me call you back," Shadae ended the call before stepping closer to examine my injuries. "What happened? Are you okay?" Shadae quizzed, pulling me from the car.

I locked my doors and followed Shadae inside. She led me over to the couch and ran through the house for a few moments before returning to me. "What the fuck, Banks? You left here less than an hour ago, what happened?" Gently pressing a wet rag against my split lip, Shadae looked at me with pity and handed me an ice pack. "Here, put this on your eye, it will help reduce swelling because that thing is about to be swollen shut in a minute. Are you going to tell me what happened?"

"Look man, help me without all these damn questions," I grumbled, snatching the ice pack from her grasp.

Shadae hopped to her feet and folded her arms across her chest. "You came over here asking me for help, not the other way around. Actually, get the fuck out, go find somebody else to doctor on your ass. I've been more that nice and understanding towards you and that fucked up attitude, I already told you that me and my baby don't need you or your bullshit. Bye!"

Shadae stood and stormed over to the door, opening it up for me. Leaning my head back on her couch, I stared up at the ceiling. Today was an emotional rollercoaster for sure. I started the day sulking about the baby and then I took Shadae to the doctor's office and experienced love at first sight when that ultrasound image appeared on the monitor. That moment was probably the highlight of my life, then the shit with Zalana brought me right back down to the pits of hell. I wasn't trying to run her life, but she was my baby sister and I only wanted what was best for her. Something in me told me that nigga she was dealing with wasn't that.

"I apologize for snapping on you like that. I just have a lot on my mind, Shadae," I lamented. "I'm sorry about everything I've said to you out of pocket before. We are a family now and I like the sound of that. I'm looking at life clearly now and that's a part of why I chose to come here. My mind fucked up and I'm out here doing dumb shit in all aspects of my life. Please don't put me out Shadae, I apologize."

Rolling her eyes, Shadae slammed her door shut then reclaimed her seat next to me. She silently resumed cleaning the blood off of my face and I placed the ice pack over my eye.

"If you plan to be here for a while, I need you to take a shower, you got dirt all over you and it's getting on my couch," Shadae expressed, breaking the silence after a while.

"Alright, let me go grab my basketball shorts out of the car," I stood and pain coursed through my body in all directions, causing me to wince in pain.

"It's okay, worry about taking your clothes off and I'll go grab your bag."

"Nah, I got it," I assured her. "I ain't that beat up."

"If you say so," Shadae chuckled.

I went outside and retrieved my Nike duffle bag that I kept in the trunk for when I played basketball. There was a change of clothes in there that would hold me over. When I re-entered the house I locked the door and headed towards the bathroom. Shadae was seated on the edge of the garden tub with a package of Dr Teal's epsom salt in her hand. She sprinkled a generous amount into the water and stood to place it underneath the bathroom sink.

"The epsom salt will help relieve some of your body aches and soreness."

"Thank you, Shadae," I gripped her hands before Shadae could leave and placed my hand on her stomach. "For keeping the baby, for allowing me to be here on this journey with you, and taking care of me today."

"You're welcome. I just want to make one thing clear, we are co-parenting and I'm helping you out because I genuinely care about you. Not because I'm looking for you to sweep me off of my feet and say you want to be with me."

"Damn, so I don't have a chance at all?"

"Not at the moment," she smiled shyly and I knew her words didn't match her true feelings. Leaning down, I planted a kiss on Shadae's lips and she didn't fight it. "You can play hard to get but I'm willing to put in the work to tear that wall down." A gentle thump against my hand caused me to jump back.

"What was that?"

"I think that was the baby kicking, it's the first time I felt it but the doctor said that I would feel the baby kicks soon now that I'm eighteen weeks," Shadae reminded me.

Stepping closer to Shadae again, I placed my hand on her stomach. Excited to feel the kick again, I rubbed around the circumference of her stomach. "If that's what that was, then I can only assume that the baby is on my side and we need to at least try to see what would happen."

Shadae took a deep breath before exiting the bathroom. Maybe my mother was right, being a family was the move. I wanted to be here for Shadae and the baby every step of the way and present for all of their milestones.

CHAPTER TWENTY-TWO

Zalana

"*Z*alana," Streetz gently nudged my shoulder and my eyes fluttered open.

We were parked outside of a beautiful resort and my eyes darted towards the time on the LCD display. It was a little after seven o'clock and I was feeling energized after that long drive. I don't know when I fell asleep but I needed that nap after waking up early and working on my studio.

"Where are we?" I inquired, observing my surroundings.

"Key Largo," he responded. "I only have one rule before we get in here and start our trip. Put that phone up and enjoy your time with me. Ion want you on that social media shit, it takes away from the vibe. You are living it for the next twenty-four hours, not recording it. Matter fact, put that shit on airplane mode until I return you. No social media, interruptions from your family calling because I beat yo brother's ass, or yo loud ass homegirls calling to be nosey. You wanted to see me and now you got me, can you do that for me though?"

"I can do that," I nodded in agreement.

We exited the car and Streetz got us checked into the room then we went to Target to grab pajamas and essentials for the evening. When we got back to the hotel we showered together and I noticed blood behind Streetz's ear. I gently wiped the area with a rag but when we got out, I noticed the cut was bigger than I initially thought. Banks wore a ring that daddy gifted him as a child and I'm sure that's what cut Streetz. For a brief moment I felt bad for not calling to check on him but I was sure his ass was sitting in our parents' living room telling all of my business.

"Oh my God, this cut is kind of big," I noted, examining the area.

Streetz gripped my waist and snuggled his face into the crook of my neck. "Small thing to a giant." His breath against my skin was tickling me and our closeness left my yoni yearning for him. I fantasized about all the freaky shit I would do with Streetz if we crossed paths again. Here we were, it was time to act and I was bitching up... then Streetz kissed the side of my neck and all of my apprehension went out of the window.

We were fresh out of the shower, dressed in our robes, and his dick was already poking out at me. I dropped down to my knees and greeted his pretty black tool with a gentle kiss. The kiss led to me slipping his dick into my mouth, coating it with my saliva. Gripping it with both hands, I jacked his dick while focusing on the head. His hands slid through my curls until he reached the middle of my scalp. Streetz gripped a handful of my hair and forced me to look up at him. A grin slid across my face as we stared at each other while he took control fucking my throat. I fought the urge to gag because I wasn't going to bitch up now that Streetz was in my presence.

Without warning, he pulled his dick out of my mouth and snatched me off the ground. Once I was up on my feet, Streetz pushed me over to the bed and bent me over. I yelped in pleasure as he slid inside of me.

"Ewww this dick fits so perfectly. It was made for me," I moaned out.

"Oh yeah?" Streetz questioned, slapping my ass as he pulled out of me.

Before I could protest he pushed me onto the bed and took my clit into his mouth. "Ahhhhhh!" I moaned as he slid two fingers inside of me. My legs were sprawled across his shoulders as the orgasm rose in the pit of my stomach. I tried to sit up but Streetz pushed me back down and released the suction he had on my clit.

"Nah, I want you to cum on this dick," he growled, slapping my thighs. Within the blink of an eye he was filling me up with dick. The teasing that Streetz was doing tonight had my head gone. He slipped inside of me, kissing me deeply while stroking my pussy just right. My hormones were raging and I thrust my hips up to meet his strokes as I moaned into his mouth. Streetz broke the kiss and sucked on my neck, pushing me to that euphoric place. My body jerked and I pulled Streetz in deeper, desperate to feel every piece of his nine inches inside of me while I rode the much needed orgasm.

Streetz collapsed while his dick was deep inside of me and I silently panicked. "Don't tense up now. I tried to pull out, you was the one holding a nigga like I was about to leave or some shit," Streetz commented, pulling out of me. I hated how intuitive Streetz was because I wouldn't ever be able to hide shit from him. "I might have to make good on that threat to bring you home pregnant."

"I'm going to have to get on birth control messing around with you," I panted.

"You really think it's a good idea to take it there, especially after today?"

"If that was the case I wouldn't be laying next to you right now."

"I hear you," Streetz replied, pulling me into his chest. "I'm proud of you for spending your money wisely. Your studio looks amazing, it fits your boisterous personality. I can't wait to see you dancing with the girls instead of on Instagram all damn day."

"How do you know all of that?"

"I have my ways. I told you I did my research."

"Okay Mr. I did my research, since you didn't pull out, I need to pee and take a shower. You coming with me?"

"You gone let me fuck again?"

I grinned brightly as I stood from the bed and rushed into the bathroom.

~

We slept in this morning after a long night of fucking. To my surprise, Streetz's mean ass had a full itinerary planned for us today. We enjoyed room service for a late breakfast on our balcony that overlooked the beautiful blue water. I never visited the Florida Keys and I hated that I missed the scenery on the drive down here. However, I was going to sulk up every second of it now that we were here.

After breakfast we went kayaking. That wasn't my first choice for the day, but it was something for Streetz. He was the silent introvert type and the experience was so serene and intimate. Streetz was dead serious about no phones during the trip and locked both of our devices in the hotel safe. Alone with Streetz in the middle of nature, I know from the outside looking in, I seemed dumb as fuck. This nigga had a rap sheet as long as my femur bone and I didn't have my phone on me to call for help if anything went awry. However, the vibe between us was pure bliss.

I enjoyed kayaking with Streetz but the next portion of the day was catered to me. We embarked on a sightseeing boat tour where we were able to visit a few local restaurants and bars by boat. In the presence of Streetz, I was comfortable enough to drink but I didn't want to get sloppy drunk. We stopped at three restaurants and I was on my third drink while feeling good. At the third restaurant we secured entrees. I ordered the California rolls and an island taco while Streetz got some wings and fries. Seated on the boat eating our food with a glass of wine, I felt good as fuck. Then the daunting thoughts of our trip ending tomorrow invaded my mind. As the sound of the waves crashing against the boat filled the atmosphere, I decided to break the silence.

"So what happens after this? I don't want to go back to Tampa and you disappear on me again," I posed my question before sticking another piece of sushi in my mouth.

Streetz pushed his plate to the side and cleaned his hands before responding. "I never disappeared on you. That would imply that we never held a discussion about what was going to happen next. I was honest with you in the A and told you that I didn't think this shit between us was a good idea. Look what happened, I had to beat yo brotha's ass. He probably told your people and maybe even the police and shit."

Sighing deeply, I wished I could've checked my phone to see if any of those things occurred. "My brother isn't the type to go to the police and he probably didn't tell my parents because he won't want to seem weak."

"Yeah, I hear you. How you think your pops would feel about you dating a convicted felon? I told you I did my research, he used to work for the district attorney's office. Yo people want you with a different type of nigga."

"What about what I want? I want *you*. Maybe I should've left you the fuck alone because you are really making me feel unwanted."

"Fuck yeah I want you," Streetz declared then got silent again. "I just don't want to bring drama into your life. Plus I can't afford to take another loss."

"What does that mean? How do you equate dealing with me to taking another loss?"

"You wanna be in this shit for real, Zalana? When I say I'm not taking another loss, I mean that. If we start some shit, it's gone be some forever shit. I can't lose another person that I let close to my heart."

"As long as you treat me right, you won't lose me," I assured him.

Pushing my food to the side, I was done eating and it was time to process that this nigga didn't want to be fucked up with me. Staring out into the water, I felt Streetz ease up behind me. Streetz's strong arms embraced me in a hug from behind and he gently nibbled on my ear.

A seagull swooped down and pecked at my hair, causing me to jump back and ruin the moment. Streetz swatted his hand and the seagull flew away. Before Streetz could pull me into his embrace again the bird swooped down again. "He is probably after my hair because the products I use have pomegranate and honey in them."

"Ion give a fuck what he wants he better..."

The seagull swooped down again before Streetz could complete his sentence. Streetz released the grip he had on me and punched the seagull in the side of the head. The bird plopped down on the deck of the boat and flopped around for a few moments. "Oh my God!" My hands flew to my mouth because I thought Streetz killed him. The bird was dazed for a moment before it took flight much slower than it did before.

"Fuck that bird and anybody else that wanna play with you or what we are building. That's how I'm coming behind you every time; no matter who, when, or where. You sure this what you want *forever*, Zalana?"

This fool might've just punched a seagull but the bird was pecking away at my head. "I'd be a fool not to acknowledge that being with you would come with a certain set of challenges but I'm prepared to weather any storms we may face."

"It's official then, Zalana and Streetz against the world," Streetz announced, scooping me off of my feet. I wrapped my legs around him and leaned down to kiss his handsome face.

"Zalana and Streetz against the world," I squealed.

CHAPTER TWENTY-THREE

Streetz

*A*fter beating Banks' ass and driving to Key Largo with Zalana fast asleep in the passenger seat, I knew it would be hard to remove myself from her life again. I enjoyed everything about Zalana, from that goofy ass laugh to the way she sucked my dick just right. When Dro called me on Wednesday, I was on my way to grab something to eat. We didn't chop it up like that on a regular basis, he was a cool ass nigga but I kept everybody at arm's length. The altercation with Zalana's bitch ass brother Banks was exactly why I kept my distance. I ain't been home from prison for a full six months and I wasn't trying to end up in a cell again. After the conversation over the water yesterday, it was whatever.

The last thing I wanted to do was return to the city. I enjoyed my uninterrupted time with Zalana. When I passed the phone back to Zalana, that shit was going off back to back. Surprisingly, she turned that shit back off and didn't address anyone until we were approaching the county line. Now it was back to the real world as I heard Zalana's demanding ass mama barking on her through the phone.

"Okay, mama. I'm coming straight to the house," she stated before pausing for a moment. "I love you too. See you soon." She disconnected the call and turned to me. "I'm so sorry, I know that I planned to take you to the studio and show you around but my family is having a dinner. Banks is having a baby and this is the first time we are meeting the family. My parents live in Ruskin so we will pass their house soon. You can drop me off and my brother will take me home."

"Just put the address in," I instructed, passing Zalana the phone.

Fifteen minutes later I pulled into the driveway of a nice ass house with a perfectly manicured lawn. A beautiful woman who resembled Zalana was at the door grabbing an Amazon package off the welcome mat. She spotted my car, her eyes squinted on me as she approached my whip. She placed her right hand against her forehead, shielding her eyes from the sun to obtain a better view.

"Let me go before my mama's nosey ass comes over here to interrogate you," Zalana announced.

She was too late though. As soon as she opened the door her mama was talking. "Zalana, bring your guy friend inside so we can meet him. I no longer want you hiding who you are with and where you are going after everything we've been through. You promised you would be open and honest from now on, then you disappeared yesterday and didn't answer the phone."

"Alright ma," Zalana rolled her eyes before looking in my direction. "Can you please stay for dinner?"

"Depends, does your mama know how to cook?"

"Even better, my parents have a personal chef and she throws down in the kitchen," Zalana chirped, licking her lips. "I know that you will enjoy whatever it is she prepared for dinner. Oh, and I know that Banks didn't tell my parents what happened because my phone would've been filled with messages talking shit. My grandfather temporarily moved back after everything that happened with me so I'm sure he will be in attendance as well."

"I'll stay for dinner but you're coming back to my place afterwards. I ain't ready to let you go anyways."

"Come on Zalana and company, Pamela was already moving the food to the table," her mother urged.

I opened the door and exited the car behind Zalana. "Ma, this is Streetz... Streetz, this is my mother, Zenobia."

"Streetz," she cringed before turning to me. "Honey, what's your real name?"

"Samuel," I extended my hand to embrace her.

"Oh no, I'm a hugger," Zenobia waved my hand off before pulling me into a firm hug.

"It's nice to meet you, Samuel."

"Likewise," I nodded, pulling the box from her hand. "I can carry that for you."

"Handsome and a gentleman, I'm loving this for Zalana already." Zenobia hiccuped and covered her mouth, I knew then that she was twisted or on her way there.

We entered the home and Zenobia instructed me to put the box down by the front door before following Zalana into the bathroom to wash my hands. Stepping inside, Zalana closed the bathroom door and caressed my shoulders. "Relax," she cooed.

"You better stop that shit before I sit you on yo people's bathroom sink and fuck the shit out of you to help me relax."

"Okay, I'll keep my hands to myself until we get back to your place," Zalana giggled.

It took a few minutes to wash our hands and we joined the rest of her family in the dining room where everyone was already seated. The first face I noticed in the room was Shadae, grinning like a Cheshire cat in the seat next to Banks. He smiled just as big as Shadae while rubbing her belly with his healing black eye on full display. I processed that shit and moved to pull Zalana's chair out but Mr. Peterson hopped up prepared to cause a scene. Prior to this moment, I always said that I would snap that nigga's trachea through his spine if we crossed paths again, but I was on my best behavior with Zalana by my side.

"What is *he* doing here?"

Zenobia pulled her lips away from the wine glass and looked between me and Mr. Peterson. "How do you two know each other?"

"Just some people that I used to know," I explained, claiming my seat next to Zalana. I guess Banks recognized me now because he was mugging me too. Banks' disdain for me left him blind to the hurtful stare Shadae was giving me from his side. I knew I shouldn't have crossed this line with Zalana but we were too far to go back now. Up until this point, I had no idea that Shadae and Banks were dealing with each other. As long as Shadae didn't make this shit messy, I wouldn't fuck her life up, and I'd mind my business. Zalana glanced at me with questioning eyes and I leaned in to whisper in her ear. "I'll tell you about it later." My head swiveled towards the door and I spotted a pregnant woman entering the dining room with a tray of lobster tails. The shit looked delicious and I was ready to see what these boujie motha fucka's personal chef was hittin' for.

"Well, dinner is already not going according to plan so I'm going to step outside with Zalana's guest."

"For what, dad?" Zalana protested.

"So we can formally meet and have a word. You didn't bother to introduce the gentleman so I'll do things my way."

"Oh come on Ezra, I was about to make the introductions but I..."

Ezra glared at Zenobia, ceasing her words instantly. Slightly baffled by the request, I hesitantly stood to my feet and followed Ezra outside. My guards were up and I was ready for whatever. I just prayed I wouldn't have to put Zalana's daddy on his head during our first interaction. When we reached the front door Ezra motioned for me to step outside and I complied. As soon as I stepped in front of him, I felt the sensation of cold steel against the back of my head. "What kind of sick shit is this? You were involved in Zalana's kidnapping and now you're trying to court her? Sitting in her family home like everything is cool?"

"Huh?" My eyebrows raised, intrigued at his words while simultaneously playing dumb. I wasn't expecting this shit and I needed a brief moment to gather my thoughts.

"Listen lil nigga, I know you had something to do with Zalana's kidnapping so now I just want you to leave here and lose her phone number."

"I ain't going to be able to do that so you better stand on business and pull that trigger now. If not, I'mma go back in there and tell ya daughter that *you* were behind her kidnapping. The *only* reason you could possibly know I was there and I'm still walking free is if *you* paid them niggas to snatch your own flesh and blood."

To Be Continued

Make sure you join my Facebook group: https://www.facebook.com/groups/keesbookbees
Mailing list: https://bit.ly/2RTP3EV

FOLLOW ME ON SOCIAL MEDIA

Instagram: https://instagram.com/authorlakia
Facebook: https://www.facebook.com/AuthorLakia
Facebook: https://www.facebook.com/kiab9o
TikTok: https://www.tiktok.com/@authorlakia

Join me in my Facebook group for giveaways, book discussions and a few laughs and gags! Maybe a few sneak peeks in the future.
https://www.facebook.com/groups/keesbookbees
Or search Kee's Book Bees

ALSO BY LAKIA

The Rise Of A Gold Mouth Boss

A Cold Summer With My Hitta

Soul Of Fire

Sweet Licks (1-3)

Riding The Storm With A Street King

Running Off On My Baby Daddy At Christmas Time

Crushing On The Plug Next Door (1-2)

.

Made in the USA
Middletown, DE
05 July 2023

34598471R00097